WORLDS OF IF SCIENCE FICTION

FEBRUARY, 2024
Vol. 1, No. 1
Issue 177

FROM THE EDITORS:
Justin T. O'Conor Sloane, Editor-in-Chief
Jean-Paul L. Garnier, Deputy Editor-in-Chief

Editor-in-Chief Justin T. O'Conor Sloane
Deputy Editor-in-Chief Jean-Paul L. Garnier
Science Editor Dr. Daniel Pomarède

Contributing Editor Robert Silverberg
Design & Layout by F. J. Bergmann
https://worldsofifmagazine.com/

FROM THE EDITORS

Dear Reader,

THANK YOU FOR BEING HERE! The relaunch of *Worlds of IF* science fiction magazine has been an invigorating blur of multitudinous moving parts and the excitement of equally multitudinous possibilities and developments. I had originally intended to write a lengthy history of *Worlds of IF,* but as our work progressed, I realized that was just not necessary. You can read all about it pretty much anywhere, including in my introduction on the *Worlds of IF* website.

Instead, what has very deeply inspired my editorial efforts is the exceptionally high level of interest and enthusiasm that the relaunch of this venerable magazine has generated—and from all quarters, too! Further, the special timing of this relaunch. And finally, my musings on the aesthetics of time, reconnection, and continuum. We live in a society continually effervescing with different interests, perspectives, and motivations—interweaving the new and the old. Things come back around, often in cycles of two or three decades, give or take. And here we are. The unifying power of shared interests, like science fiction, provides a vibrant cultural forum in which like-minded individuals arrive independently at a shared experience of the world. I see the revival of *Worlds of IF* as being the reopening of one particular door to a shared community of culture, history, and literary enrichment. Like with any remake of a beloved classic, it brings back fond memories, usually evoking a sense of nostalgia, and stirring up some excitement. It can also provide a pleasant sense of continuum—that what once was, will be again. Deputy EIC Jean-Paul was at a con in SoCal recently promoting the magazine and mentioned to me people's genuinely happy response to news of the relaunch.

That I am writing this editorial in the relaunch of *Worlds of IF* is contextually the very embodiment of the idea of the generational starship as I envisioned it to be when naming this publishing company. *Worlds of IF* is a ship that launched over seventy years ago and now, reprovisioned, carries in it generations of science fiction passengers onward through the literary cosmos. That luminaries in the starlit field of science fiction are on board to continue in this shared journey imbues this project with a very special energy and fills me with a profound sense of joy—and I genuinely hope that it does for you as well. The excitement surrounding this project has been far greater than anything I had anticipated. That, in and of itself, has been a rich and largely unexpected reward of this venture.

The timing of this relaunch has been most auspicious, as the Great Gray Guard— that illustrious generation that was born around the end of the Gernsback Era, with their formative years during the Campbell Era and the Golden Age of Science Fiction, and beginning to make their bones during the transitional period of the '50s that Bob Silverberg views as also being a golden age, and then into the New Wave of science fiction—who made SF what it is, are still with us! Not only that, but they also continue to be actively involved in the realm of SF! We are fortunate that this is so. I respect their efforts and their contributions immensely.

This magazine is bringing back something that people want. Maybe even something that people need. I have come to realize that what we want can be just as meaningful, and just as important (or more so), to our spiritual sustenance as that which we may in fact need—like a root canal, or car insurance. Neither of which gets me out of bed in the morning. Joie de vivre is probably worth more than all of the doctors and their prescriptions in enlivening our quality of life, our mental and physical health, and our longevity. *Worlds of IF* provides joy of life!

I also firmly believe that science fiction can serve as a living blueprint for the betterment of humanity. It has rightly been called the literature of ideas. Science fiction is the ultimate laboratory of thought experiments. Through it, we can envision radical new worlds for the human experience to flourish in, or fail, try out all sorts of systems and approaches, speculating on their viability and the possible outcomes. Experiment at will. It costs nothing to do so and we just might stumble upon some great answers, maybe even to questions that we haven't thought to ask yet. Science fiction can redirect our trajectory and reshape the future that we will come to build. Time and again, science fiction announces that which becomes science fact. Think Heinlein and the cell phone; a modest example perhaps, but illustrative. If we can imagine it, we can build it. So too, the future that we deserve (I know, that's open to interpretation).

Various aspects of *Worlds of IF* have always appealed to me. To begin with, the cover art! This magazine has very often had the best cover art of any SF magazine on the market—and this tradition will continue. When Clifford Hong revived this magazine in 1986, Bob Eggleton's art was on its cover. Now, almost 40 years later, Bob's art is on the cover again! Bob is a legend in the world of SFF art. I love this continuum. *Worlds of IF* was known to be a publication that embraced working with new writers and experimenting with new approaches in the genre. Editor Frederik Pohl had a real blast doing so, and in the process won the magazine three Hugos, outselling *Galaxy* in the process. That commitment to the new will continue, wholeheartedly, and is already on display in this issue—the established and the not so established both share these pages. That's exciting! Most importantly, a true diversity of voices will be presented herein—and that's very exciting! Furthermore, we will be keeping some departments that have long existed within the magazine, like Science Briefs, and Hue and Cry, while adding new departments, like one I'm calling Sidereal Time, which will cover interesting topics relating to the super genre of speculative fiction. Finally, we are, at least for the time being, keeping the traditional digest-sized format for this magazine, so that it may seamlessly grace your shelves with the issues that have come before—Jean-Paul insisted on this point.

Attract talented people who share a vision and you are well ahead of the game even before having started. Here are the co-editors that I am honored to work with.

Anybody will tell you: choose a partner in any endeavor that brings strengths to your weaknesses and further amplifies your potential. Jean-Paul L. Garnier does exactly that as deputy editor-in-chief. He is that rare breed of individual who can juggle a variety of practical concerns, like aspects of the publishing business, with tremendous efforts of hypercreativity—and not miss a beat in either domain. He also serves as a bit of a cognitive referee for me, as I strike off into various and sometimes remote territories of the mind, following the will-o'-the-wisp of some idea, reminding me or informing me of things that I usually don't want to hear about. Like costs. Schedules. Contracts. Planning. Word count. Advertising & marketing. Format. Spreadsheets. Did I mention costs? More importantly though, Jean-Paul contributes lots and lots of really great ideas, which I always want to hear about. Combine all of that with the preternatural abilities of a mountain goat in traversing cliffs of near-vertical workloads and you'll better understand why he has already accomplished so much in the field of science fiction. As well, we favor different flavors of science fiction, the resulting blend is robust and should have something in it that appeals to everyone. I'm more of a traditionalist in my SF sensibilities. I suppose that one might consider me a Campbellian of sorts, while Jean-Paul forwards the cutting-edge, weird, genre-bending-blending-and-blurring stuff. We had another discussion about it not long before wrapping on content inclusion for this magazine. I think the conversation bears noting as it is illustrative of the evolution of science fiction and how that plays out in a relaunched classic SF magazine, and again, one known for experimentation and trying new things on for size. I mentioned a few of Jean-Paul's excellent selections in our conversation, but focused on one poem in particular. A wonderful piece of work, certainly, but one that I do not consider to be science fiction. Speculative, yes. The poem reflects the new and ever-expanding horizon of SF&F. It's all about perspective and Jean-Paul's rationale is strong, anti-stagnation kung-fu. We can't be stuck in any one mindset regarding what we deem to be sufficiently SF if we want to grow with the times and be sustainable. Nor do we position ourselves as arbiters of what SF can or should be. We are quite simply the editors. Jean-Paul reminded me that Damon Knight (once an editor of *If*, as I'm sure you know), said something roughly along the lines of SF being whatever you point to when you say hey, that's SF. There is no one clear definition of the genre. I'm also reminded of a well-known SF magazine that found itself facing challenges in their volume of sales and submissions respectively, due to a very strict in-house definition of what should be considered SF. They broadened their perspective, loosening their self-imposed strictures, and bloomed—in the process, scandalizing some readers with an especially risqué piece about an intelligent orangutan, which, of course, did wonders for both sales and submissions! So there you have it, folks, we are a classic SF mag relaunching itself on the parapet of the new, atop a structure long since built, celebrating and embracing both the old and the new. We look forward to the journey ahead.

Dr. Daniel Pomarède is one of the world's foremost cosmographers. He is a staff scientist at the Institute of Research into the Fundamental Laws of the Universe, CEA Paris-Saclay University and holds a Ph.D. in particle physics and cosmology. Daniel's h-index is 89, which is truly exceptional. Before the honor of having made his acquaintance, I knew of his co-discovery of the South Pole Wall. I had read all about it in the news and was genuinely fascinated. It was awe-inspiring. That a cosmic structure of such glorious and giddying magnitude could have existed for so long without us knowing about it, and in our own backyard, simply boggled my mind—still does. I found it to be one of the most exciting of scientific discoveries and discussed it with my secondary-school classes. Later, I learned of Daniel's co-discoveries of Laniakea, our home supercluster of galaxies, and of the Dipole Repeller and the Cold Spot Repeller, both large cosmic voids. Very recently, he co-discovered Ho'oleilana, which is quite possibly the remnant of a Baryon Acoustic Oscillation. I am very pleased that Daniel is on board as the science editor. He is able to write in a manner that takes complex scientific concepts and makes them engaging and accessible for the rest of us. I hope that you enjoy Daniel's expansive essay in this issue.

What can I say about Robert Silverberg

Aqua, Rodney Matthews

that hasn't been said already? He is an SF legend. Pure and simple. I can tell you that I am a big fan of his work. He's been on everyone's must-read list of top science fiction authors for a very, very long time now. And he's won all of the big awards—and then he went back and won them all again. It's an honor to have Bob on board as contributing editor. Enjoy his story in this issue, "The Pain Peddlers." In an email conversation with Bob, I mentioned that the story sounded like the next big Netflix reality show. He replied that he had once written in reference to the story that he may well have invented the concept of reality television. Hard to argue that point. His story was published in *Galaxy*, the sister publication of *Worlds of IF*, in 1969—many decades before reality television became a phenomenon of popular culture. Once again, science fiction manifests an uncanny knack for predicting the future. Getting back to the aforementioned beauty of the continuum, I'm overjoyed that Bob gets a hoot out of being published in this magazine again after so many decades and in serving as its contributing editor now, too! He also gets a kick out of me basically doing the same stuff as T. O'Conor Sloane at *Amazing Stories*. Bob's a big fan of *Amazing,* and he

has its full run from the '20s and '30s, maybe beyond that, too, but we just talked about that era of the magazine. Being in contact with Bob has further energized and inspired me in this venture.

Bob's immediately forthcoming book is the stand-alone edition of the novella *The Secret Sharer,* which Subterranean Press will be publishing shortly (as of this writing). The book just before that, *Living in the Future,* is a collection of Bob's essays from the magazine *Asimov's Science Fiction* and was published recently by NESFA Press.

Be on the lookout for the second issue of *Worlds of IF*. It is already shaping up to be riotously good! Rodney Matthews, the legendary British science fiction & fantasy artist, is not only providing the cover art, but his is also the featured artist interview, by yours truly. The art is perfectly stunning, and the interview is full of insight, warmth, and wonder.

Safe travels, children of the stars …

Cheers,
Justin T. O'Conor Sloane,
Editor-in-Chief
Worlds of IF Science Fiction magazine
Austin-Round Rock, TX
2024

WORLDS OF IF MAGAZINE HAS a rich history in SF. It was often known as the younger sibling of *Galaxy* magazine, and was eventually assimilated into it, but because of this it was a place for editors to take chances on new authors and try out experimental approaches. We intend to keep this spirit alive. Like all things in life, science fiction is constantly evolving, and I do not view it as my job to define SF, but rather to encourage its growth and expansion. As a medium that often deals in the future, I find it important to nurture its movement into the future, to find new voices, and new ways of telling stories. For literature is not a stagnant process, but rather an unfolding emotional history, our future history. SF is a place where we can dream, look forwards or backwards, warn of disastrous futures, and conjure positive outcomes. SF is a testing ground for new ideas and a place for us to reconsider that which has come before. And speaking of reviewing the past, visit **archive.org** to view and read scans of back issues of *Worlds of IF;* it's a treasure trove of fun science fiction, not all amazing but filled with hidden gems.

IF has a long lineage of incredible editors, many names that will be familiar to fans of SF. Looking at the list of previous editors I find myself in awe. Difficult shoes to fill to be sure. Mr. Sloane and I couldn't be more pleased to join these folks in support of our field of literature. We have different tastes and different approaches about how to do things, and I view this as a unique strength. Since we have different methods in running a magazine and selecting stories, I believe that this will lead us into a place of balance and bring readers a more well-rounded magazine which is fun to read and thought-provoking.

It is a strange time to be launching a magazine, let alone reviving one that has already had its ups and downs. Changes in the publishing landscape have caused many excellent magazines to fold in recent months due to price increases, difficulties in distribution, and social media ceasing to be a dependable way to stay in touch with readers. These are all grave challenges to running a successful magazine and I am deeply saddened to see some of our peers fall victim to these changes. It is also an exciting time to be launching a magazine, because change is always inevitable, and we work in a field that is constantly adapting and finding new ways to thrive. I wholeheartedly believe that we will find creative ways to navigate these changes and find sustainable new methods for supporting authors and reaching readers. Our love of science fiction will guide the way, and as obsessive fans of science fiction we are prepared to look toward the future with resolve and perseverance. One of the things that gives me hope in these strange times is the tremendous amount of quality writing that is being produced these days, both from emerging authors and those we are already familiar with, and for this reason I plan to focus on curating story and poetry selections that are multigenerational, multifaceted, challenging, fun, and in constant motion. It is my opinion that most readers read widely and do not care for their tastes to be pigeonholed. That's how I read, anyway. It is my hope that in every issue of *Worlds of IF* you will find something unexpected and fresh, alongside classic forms of storytelling. There are countless ways to tell a story and I'm excited to be seeking innovation and mold-breaking new forms.

We live in times of great uncertainty

about the future, an uncertainty that has always been with us and caused states of fear and confusion. What better way to explore this aspect of humanity than in the forward-looking field of science fiction? We live in a time that demands new ideas, a rethinking of the past, and a splash of much needed hope. This is what science fiction is all about! So, writers and readers, let's dream alternate futures together and through art manifest those outcomes which we find desirable and fruitful for all. We must first dream these realities before we can materialize them, and our dream is spread through the sharing of ideas because writing is a form of technology that makes telepathy possible. How else can we enter the minds of others and learn empathy through these unique visions?

I cannot claim to know what the future of science fiction is, let alone the future of our species, but I know that progress and innovation always begins with the dreamers. And *Worlds of IF* is a place for dreamers, a place for the proliferation of wild, radical, and fresh ideas. But it is also a place for fun, after all it is important that we create a future which is not only better for all, but also enjoyable. The human spirit must be allowed the freedom to dream, we must be like Mae Jemison and dance when we arrive at the stars, for what is a future devoid of beauty. *Worlds of IF* is a place to be serious and to play, a place to think and a place to escape. There is no reason we can't have the best of both worlds. For everything awesome begins with the question: What *IF*?

Jean-Paul L. Garnier,
Deputy Editor-in-Chief
Worlds of IF Science Fiction magazine
Joshua Tree, CA
2024

NEW ADVENTURES THIS SPRING FROM BAEN BOOKS

NEW FANTASY AND SF STORIES WITH A HARD-BOILED NOIR TWIST

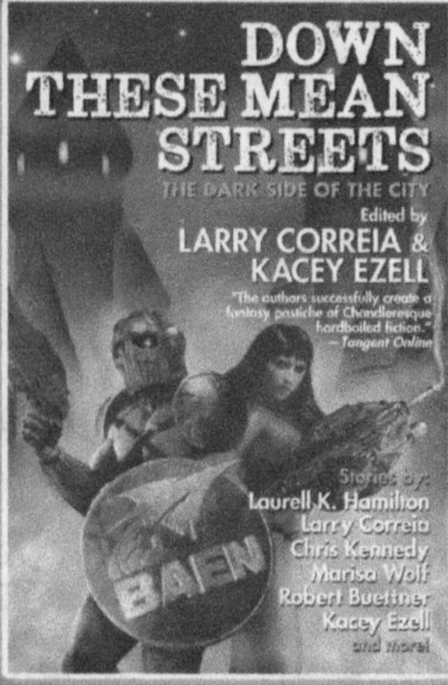

ON SALE JANUARY

FIRST CONTACT ON THE LIMITLESS AND LAWLESS FRONTIER

ON SALE FEBRUARY

A HIGH STAKES JAUNT SEQUEL TO A DRAGON-AWARD WINNING NOVEL

ON SALE MARCH

A NEW NOVEL IN THE NEW YORK TIMES BEST-SELLING HONORVERSE

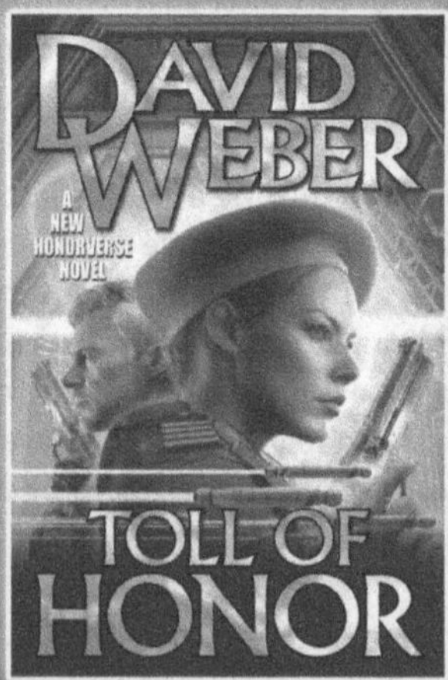

ON SALE APRIL

For free sample chapters and more visit www.baen.com.

Our Place on the Map of the Universe

Dr. Daniel Pomarède

To Steal a Battleship, Rodney Matthews

I AM A COSMOGRAPHER—literally a cartographer of the Cosmos. With a gang of a few others, we use the information imprinted in the velocities of galaxies to construct a map of the Universe.

In the prevailing theory of the Big Bang Universe and by virtue of the Cosmological Principle, the cosmos should be uniform and isotropic, that is, having the same average properties everywhere and in every direction. However, in its very first instants, quantum fluctuations, acting as primordial seeds, have given rise to what would become the elements of the cosmic cartography we observe today: planets, stars, galaxies, groups of galaxies, galaxy clusters, galaxy superclusters, walls and filaments separating voids, the whole of it organized in a gigantic architecture called the Cosmic Web. This web is composed of the ordinary stuff we, and the familiar astrophysical luminous objects, are made of. Yet it also harbors the mysterious Dark Matter that is known to be dominant in the distribution of matter in the Universe. So, how are we able to map this complex and, to some extent, elusive structure?

Over the course of their lifetime, galaxies are subject to two antagonistic phenomena: on one side, as an inheritance of the Big Bang initial singularity and the resulting expansion of the Universe, they are pushed away one from the others with a velocity that is, according to the Hubble's Law, proportional to their relative distances. It proceeds as if galaxies were caught in a flow, the so-called Hubble Flow, making them recede from each other. And, on the other side, they are subject to the force of Gravitation, a universal attractive force of infinite range, that make structures collapse on themselves, and galaxies congregate in various ways, following streams of matters we call Cosmic Flows. By separating these two phenomena, we are able to isolate the contribution of the gravitational sources that cause galaxy motions, infer the three-dimensional distribution of these sources, and hence build a Map. The data needed for this research are collected on some of the greatest astronomical instruments on Earth, such as the radio telescopes of Green Bank in the U.S., Arecibo in Puerto

9

Rico, and Parkes in Australia, and in space with the Hubble and Spitzer telescopes.

So, what is it that we have mapped so far? Before going extragalactic, let us review our inner galactic situation. Our Home planet, Earth, the pale blue dot, is a member of the Solar System, orbiting its central star, the Sun. This star, one among the several hundred billion stars making up the Milky Way galaxy, a barred spiral galaxy, is located within one of its minor spiral arms called the Orion Arm, a safe place at a distance of about 30,000 light-years from the crowded galactic center, where a supermassive black hole, Sagittarius A*, is devouring the unfortunate stars that might approach it. As peripheral a location this might be, still we are immersed in a galactic disk-like structure, filled with stars, opaque dust clouds, star-forming regions, molecular clouds. These represent an observational challenge for what cosmography is concerned with, making it impossible to completely map the Milky Way galaxy, especially in the region hidden behind the galactic center, and to directly observe the extragalactic Universe in the continuation of this disk-like structure, the so-called "Zone of Galactic Obscuration" or "Zone of Avoidance." Though this zone is not observed directly, our research program is able to map in an indirect fashion the structures, or the absence of structures (voids), which might be lurking within, thanks to the influence they exert on our mass tracers: the velocities of galaxies.

Now we are ready to leave our Home galaxy and embark for an intergalactic journey. The first starry islands we encounter are the satellite galaxies of the Milky Way: the Large Magellanic Cloud and the Small Magellanic Cloud that southern earthlings can see with the naked eye, or the Sagittarius Dwarf and the Sextans Dwarf Spheroidal, and a few dozens more. Their formation history, orbits, interactions with our galaxy, are a source of wonder and active research for cosmologists. Pursuing our journey beyond this swarm of little galaxies, we then encounter the Andromeda Galaxy. A splendor of a galaxy, much similar to our own and hosting several hundred billions stars. Located currently at a distance of about 2.5 million light-years, it is set on a collision course with the Milky Way, with a gentle contact and merger foreseen in a few billion years. Together, Andromeda and Milky Way, and their swarm of dwarves, form the "Local Group" of galaxies. Around this group, one can draw a roughly spherical "zero-energy surface" where there is an equilibrium between gravitation and expansion: inside this surface all galaxies will merge into a single super-giant elliptical galaxy, while outside this surface, everything will recede away from us into the dark.

Carrying on our journey, we realize that the Local Group and other nearby groups of galaxies, such as the Centaurus A Group, the Messier 81 Group, or the Maffei Group, belong to a flattened structure called the "Local Sheet." This thin wall is located at the boundaries of a giant cosmic void: the "Local Void." Maybe as wide as 200 million light-years, this void expands across the Zone of Avoidance, and hence it is only recently that it has been mapped thanks to our research program. Inside this expanse, a few lonely galaxies have been spotted— Cosmologists study such peculiar galaxies, peculiar in the sense that they have not been nurtured by their environment, as opposed to the vast majority that have grown up in dense surroundings.

We then proceed 50 million light-years ahead toward a local heavyweight champion: the Virgo Cluster, where a thousand spiral and elliptical galaxies

are bound together by gravitation. This cluster of galaxies is the dominant object of a greater structure called the "Virgo Supercluster" or "Local Supercluster," a 100 million light-years wide aggregation comprising many groups of galaxies, including our own Local Group.

Onward to the next level of the Map: the Great Attractor. It is by studying the velocities of 400 elliptical galaxies that, back in the eighties, a bunch of astronomers that posterity would keep under the name of the "Seven Samurai," so as to honor their boldness, discovered the Great Attractor. This attractor is a region of space that is particularly over-dense, with the noted presence of a nest of a handful of galaxy clusters, including the Centaurus Cluster. It is a very special place on the map: a knot of the Cosmic Web, where our research has established that at least five filaments, or strands, are converging. One of them, the Virgo Strand, connects Centaurus to the Virgo Cluster. The Norma-Pavo-Indus Strand, the Southern Supercluster Strand, and the Antlia Strand all run across the Zone of Avoidance to connect with the Southern galactic sky. Back in 2014, we discovered the Laniakea supercluster of galaxies. This structure appeared in our map as a volume inside which cosmic flows converge onto a unique attractor, the Great

Attractor, and outside which these flows converge on either of three other more distant attractors. Our galaxy is found to be located inside this volume, in a peripheral region, in effect making Laniakea our Home supercluster of galaxies. 500 million light-years in size, this supercluster is the largest fully mapped entity to which we belong. We gave it a Hawaiian name, built on the contraction of the terms lani: sky, heaven and akea: broad, wide, spacious, immeasurable, so as to honor the culture of the Polynesian navigators, who by their knowledge of stars and oceanic flows, where able to travel on the vast expanses of the Pacific Ocean, connecting the three vertices of the giant triangle formed by Hawaii, Easter Island, and New Zealand.

Let's now turn our eyes on what lies outside Laniakea. The three other attractors we mentioned earlier are associated with three neighboring superstructures: the Perseus-Pisces Supercluster, the Great Wall, and the super-heavy Shapley Concentration of Clusters, made of 28 galaxy clusters. Cosmic Voids do play an important role. Back in 2017 we published the discovery of the "Dipole Repeller," a void, at a distance of 700 million light-years in a region of the northern sky that has remained uncharted. A void has this remarkable property that it manifests itself in our three-dimensional map as a divergence in the velocity field: a point from which cosmic flows emanate on their way from under-dense to over-dense regions. So, what's going on here? It's just gravitation having its way, resulting in matter flowing from the void under-dense region, toward the over-dense regions surrounding it, the dense cores and filaments and walls of the Cosmic Web. The void acts effectively as a repeller, and it was found that the Dipole Repeller contributes in a significant manner to the velocity of our Local Group of Galaxies. Its name is a reference to the dipole effect this velocity implies on the cosmic microwave background radiation, the relic light from an early stage of the Universe. Another such major and influential void, dubbed the "Cold Spot Repeller," was found at a distance of one billion light-years, and in a direction coincident with the coldest point observed in the map of the relic radiation, hence its name.

Finally, our map revealed the existence of a gigantic, large-scale structure, a 1.4 billion light-years galactic filament, hidden behind the obscured regions on the fringes of the Zone of Avoidance and in the direction of the Chameleon constellation and of the South Celestial Pole. Named the South Pole Wall, this filament is shaped like an arc that embraces the southernmost frontiers of Laniakea. It is among the largest structures of the Universe.

Many other outstanding structures have been spotted by fellow cosmographers who have turned their attention to some specific and increasingly distant regions of the universe, to name a few: the Sloan Great Wall, the BOSS Great Wall, the Saraswati Supercluster, the Giant GRB (Gamma-Ray Burst) Ring, and the Giant Arc on the Sky, but that's another story.

Cosmography is a thrilling endeavor, making us in practice the descendants of the antique world cartographers, we experience the thrill of those who have explored uncharted territories and if fortune was kind enough, suddenly discovered a new land, a new continent. It feels like standing on a bridge, connecting the past of humanity's knowledge building and mapmaking, and the future of the human adventure in the cosmos. Who knows what will become of these maps: how far will they be extended and how will they be used by our own descendants?

THE PAIN PEDDLERS

Robert Silverberg

Pain is Gain.
—Greek proverb

THE PHONE BLEEPED. Northrop nudged the cut-in switch and heard Maurillo say, "We got a gangrene, chief. They're amputating tonight."

Northrop's pulse quickened at the thought of action. "What's the tab?" he asked.

"Five thousand, all rights."

"Anesthetic?"

"Natch," Maurillo said. "I tried it the other way."

"What did you offer?"

"Ten. It was no go."

Northrop sighed. "I'll have to handle it myself, I guess. Where's the patient?"

"Clinton General. In the wards."

Northrop raised a heavy eyebrow and glowered into the screen. "In the *wards?*" he bellowed. "And you couldn't get them to agree?"

Maurillo seemed to shrink. "It was the relatives, chief. They were stubborn. The old man, he didn't seem to give a damn, but the relatives—"

"Okay. You stay there. I'm coming over to close the deal," Northrop snapped. He cut the phone out and pulled a couple of blank waiver forms out of his desk, just in case the relatives backed down. Gangrene was gangrene, but ten grand was ten grand. And business was business. The networks were yelling. He had to supply the goods or get out.

He thumbed the autosecretary. "I want my car ready in thirty seconds. South Street exit."

"Yes, Mr. Northrop."

"If anyone calls for me in the next half hour, record it. I'm going to Clinton General Hospital, but I don't want to be called there."

"Yes, Mr. Northrop."

"If Rayfield calls from the network office, tell him I'm getting him a dandy. Tell him—oh, hell, tell him I'll call him back in an hour. That's all."

"Yes, Mr. Northrop."

Northrop scowled at the machine and left his office. The gravshaft took him down forty stories in almost literally no time flat. His car was waiting, as ordered, a long, sleek '08 Frontenac with bubble top. Bulletproof, of course. Network producers were vulnerable to crack-pot attacks.

He sat back, nestling into the plush upholstery. The car asked him where he was going, and he answered.

"Let's have a pep pill," he said.

A pill rolled out of the dispenser in front of him. He gulped it down. *Maurillo, you make me sick,* he thought. *Why can't you close a deal without me? Just once?*

He made a mental note. Maurillo had to go. The organization couldn't tolerate inefficiency.

☆

The hospital was an old one. It was housed in one of the vulgar green-glass architectural monstrosities so popular sixty years before, a tasteless slab-sided thing without character or grace. The main door irised and Northrop stepped through, and the familiar hospital smell hit his nostrils. Most people found it unpleasant, but not Northrop. It was the smell of dollars, for him.

The hospital was so old that it still had nurses and orderlies. Oh, plenty of mechanicals skittered up and down the corridors, but here and there a middle-aged nurse, smugly clinging to her tenure, pushed a tray of mush along, or a doddering orderly propelled a broom. In his early days on video, Northrop had done a documentary on these people, these living fossils in the hospital corridors. He had won an award for the film, with its crosscuts from baggy-faced nurses to gleaming mechanicals, its vivid presentation of the inhumanity of the new hospitals. It was a long time since Northrop had done a documentary of that sort. A different kind of show was the order of the day now, ever since the intensifiers had come in.

A mechanical took him to Ward Seven. Maurillo was waiting there, a short, bouncy little man who wasn't bouncing much now, because he knew he had fumbled. Maurillo grinned up at Northrop, a hollow grin, and said, "You sure made it fast, chief!"

"How long would it take for the competition to cut in?" Northrop countered. "Where's the patient?"

"Down by the end. You see where the curtain is? I had the curtain put up. To get in good with the heirs. The relatives, I mean."

"Fill me in," Northrop said. "Who's in charge?"

"The oldest son. Harry. Watch out for him. Greedy."

"Who isn't?" Northrop sighed. They were at the curtain, now. Maurillo parted it. All through the long ward, patients were stirring. Potential subjects for taping, all of them, Northrop thought. The world was so full of different kinds of sickness—and one sickness fed on another.

He stepped through the curtain. There was a man in the bed, drawn and gaunt, his hollow face greenish, stubbly. A mechanical stood next to the bed, with an intravenous tube running across and under the covers. The patient looked at least ninety. Knocking off ten years for the effects of illness still made him pretty old, Northrop thought.

He confronted the relatives.

There were eight of them. Five women, ranging from middle age down to teens. Three men, the oldest about fifty, the other two in their forties. Sons and daughters and nieces and granddaughters, Northrop figured.

He said gravely, "I know what a terrible tragedy this must be for all of you. A man in the prime of his life—head of a happy family…" Northrop stared at the patient. "But I know he'll pull through. I can see the strength in him."

The oldest relative said, "I'm Harry Gardner. I'm his son. You're from the network?"

"I'm the producer," Northrop said. "I don't ordinarily come in person, but my assistant told me what a great human situation there was here, what a brave person your father is…"

The man in the bed slept on. He looked bad.

Harry Gardner said, "We made an arrangement. Five thousand bucks. We wouldn't do it, except for the hospital bills. They can really wreck you."

"I understand perfectly," Northrop said in his most unctuous tones. "That's why we're prepared to raise our offer. We're well aware of the disastrous effects of hospitalization on a small family, even today, in these times of protection. And so we can offer—"

"No! There's got to be anesthetic!" It was one of the daughters, a round, drab woman with colorless thin lips. "We ain't going to let you make him suffer!"

Northrop smiled. "It would only be a moment of pain for him. Believe me. We'd begin the anesthesia immediately after the amputation. Just let us capture that single instant of—"

"It ain't right! He's old, he's got to be given the best treatment! The pain could kill him!"

"On the contrary," Northrop said blandly. "Scientific research has shown that pain is often beneficial in amputation cases. It creates a nerve block, you see, that causes a kind of anesthesia of its own, without the harmful side effects of chemotherapy. And once the danger vectors are controlled, the normal anesthetic procedures can be invoked, and—" He took a deep breath, and went rolling glibly on to the crusher, "with the extra fee we'll provide, you can give your dear one the absolute finest in medical care. There'll be no reason to stint."

Wary glances were exchanged. Harry Gardner said, "How much are you offering?"

"May I see the leg?" Northrop countered.

The coverlet was peeled back. Northrop stared.

It was a nasty case. Northrop was no doctor, but he had been in this line of work for five years, and that was long enough to give him an amateur acquaintance with disease. He knew the old man was in bad shape. It looked as though there had been a severe burn, high up along the calf, which had probably been treated only with first aid. Then, in happy proletarian ignorance, the family had let the old man rot until he was gangrenous. Now the leg was blackened, glossy, and swollen from midcalf to the ends of the toes. Everything looked soft and decayed. Northrop had the feeling that he could reach out and break the puffy toes off, one at a time.

The patient wasn't going to survive. Amputation or not, he was probably rotten to the core by this time, and if the shock of amputation didn't do him in, general debilitation would. It was a good prospect for the show. It was the kind of stomach-turning vicarious suffering that millions of viewers gobbled up avidly.

Northrop looked up and said, "Fifteen thousand if you'll allow a network-approved surgeon to amputate under our conditions. And we'll pay the surgeon's fee besides."

"Well…"

"And we'll also underwrite the entire cost of postoperative care for your father," Northrop added smoothly. "Even if he stays in the hospital for six months, we'll pay every nickel, over and above the telecast fee."

He had them. He could see the greed shining in their eyes. They were faced with bankruptcy, and he had come to rescue them, and did it matter all that much if the old man didn't have anesthetic when they sawed his leg off? He was hardly conscious even now. He wouldn't really feel a thing, not really.

Northrop produced the documents, the waivers, the contracts covering residuals and Latin-American reruns, the payment vouchers, all the paraphernalia. He sent Maurillo scuttling off for a secretary, and a few moments later a glistening mechanical was taking it all down.

"If you'll put your name here, Mr. Gardner …"

Northrop handed the pen to the eldest son. Signed, sealed, delivered.

"We'll operate tonight," Northrop said. "I'll send our surgeon over immediately. One of our best men. We'll give your father the care he deserves."

He pocketed the documents. It was done. Maybe it was barbaric to operate on an old man that way, Northrop thought, but he didn't bear the responsibility, after all. He was just giving the public what it wanted, and the public wanted spouting blood and tortured nerves. And what did it matter to the old man, really? Any experienced medic could tell you he was as good as dead. The operation wouldn't save him. Anesthesia wouldn't save him. If the gangrene didn't get him, postoperative shock would do him in. At worst, he would suffer only a few minutes under the knife, but at least his family would be free from the fear of financial ruin.

On the way out, Maurillo said, "Don't you think it's a little risky, chief? Offering to pay the hospitalization expenses, I mean?"

"You've got to gamble a little sometimes to get what you want," Northrop said.

"Yeah, but that could run to fifty, sixty thousand! What'll that do to the budget?"

Northrop shrugged. "We'll survive. Which is more than the old man will. He can't make it through the night. We haven't risked a penny, Maurillo. Not a stinking cent."

☆

Returning to the office, Northrop turned the papers on the Gardner amputation over to his assistants, set the wheels in motion for the show, and prepared to call it a day. There was only one bit of dirty work left to do. He had to fire Maurillo.

It wasn't called firing, of course. Maurillo had tenure, just like the hospital orderlies and everyone else below executive rank. It was more a demotion than anything else. Northrop had been increasingly dissatisfied with the little man's work for months, now, and today had been the clincher. Maurillo had no imagination. He didn't know how to close a deal. Why hadn't he thought of underwriting the hospitalization? *If I can't delegate responsibility to him,* Northrop told himself, *I can't use him at all.* There were plenty of other assistant producers in the outfit who'd be glad to step in.

Northrop spoke to a couple of them. He made his choice. A young fellow named Barton, who had been working on documentaries all year. Barton had done the plane-crash deal in London in the spring. He had a fine touch for the gruesome. He had been on hand at the World's Fair fire last year in Juneau. Yes, Barton was the man.

The next part was the sticky one. Northrop phoned Maurillo, even though Maurillo was only two rooms away—these things were never done in person—and said, "I've got some good news for you, Ted. We're shifting you to a new program."

"Shifting…?"

"That's right. We had a talk in here this afternoon, and we decided you were being wasted on the blood and guts show. You need more scope for your talents. So we're moving you over to *Kiddie Time.* We think you'll really blossom there. You and Sam Kline and Ed Bragan ought to make a terrific team."

Northrop saw Maurillo's pudgy face crumble. The arithmetic was getting home; over here, Maurillo was Number Two, and on the new show, a much less important one, he'd be Number Three. It was a thumping boot downstairs, and Maurillo knew it.

The mores of the situation called for Maurillo to pretend he was receiving a rare honor. He didn't play the game. He squinted and said, "Just because I didn't sign up that old man's amputation?"

"What makes you think...?"

"Three years I've been with you! Three years, and you kick me out just like that!"

"I told you, Ted, we thought this would be a big opportunity for you. It's a step up the ladder. It's—"

Maurillo's fleshy face puffed up with rage. "It's getting junked," he said bitterly. "Well, never mind, huh? It so happens I've got another offer. I'm quitting before you can can me. You can take your tenure and—"

Northrop blanked the screen.

The idiot, he thought. *The fat little idiot. Well, to hell with him!*

He cleared his desk, and cleared his mind of Ted Maurillo and his problems. Life was real, life was earnest. Maurillo just couldn't take the pace, that was all.

Northrop prepared to go home. It had been a long day.

✧

At eight that evening came word that old Gardner was about to undergo the amputation. At ten, Northrop was phoned by the network's own head surgeon, Dr. Steele, with the news that the operation had failed.

"We lost him," Steele said in a flat, unconcerned voice. "We did our best, but he was a mess. Fibrillation set in, and his heart just ran away. Not a damned thing we could do."

"Did the leg come off?"

"Oh, sure. All this was *after* the operation."

"Did it get taped?"

"They're processing it now. I'm on my way out."

"Okay," Northrop said. "Thanks for calling."

"Sorry about the patient."

"Don't worry yourself," Northrop said. "It happens to the best of us."

The next morning, Northrop had a look at the rushes. The screening was in the twenty-third floor studio, and a select audience was on hand—Northrop, his new assistant producer Barton, a handful of network executives, a couple of men from the cutting room. Slick, bosomy girls handed out intensifier helmets—no mechanicals doing the work here!

Northrop slipped the helmet on over his head. He felt the familiar surge of excitement as the electrodes descended, as contact was made. He closed his eyes. There was a thrum of power somewhere in the room as the EEG-amplifier went into action. The screen brightened.

There was the old man. There was the gangrenous leg. There was Dr. Steele, crisp and rugged and dimple-chinned, the network's star surgeon, $250,000-a-year's worth of talent. There was the scalpel, gleaming in Steele's hand.

Northrop began to sweat. The amplified brain waves were coming through the intensifier, and he felt the throbbing in the old man's leg, felt the dull haze of pain behind the old man's forehead, felt the weakness of being eighty years old and half dead.

Steele was checking out the electronic scalpel, now, while the nurses fussed around, preparing the man for the amputation. In the finished tape, there would be music, narration, all the trimmings, but now there was just a soundless series of images, and, of course, the tapped brainwaves of the sick man.

The leg was bare.

The scalpel descended.

Northrop winced as vicarious agony shot through him. He could feel the blazing pain, the brief searing hellishness as the scalpel slashed through diseased flesh and rotting bone. His whole body trembled,

17

and he bit down hard on his lips and clenched his fists and then it was over.

There was a cessation of pain. A catharsis. The leg no longer sent its pulsating messages to the weary brain. Now there was shock, the anesthesia of hyped-up pain, and with the shock came calmness. Steele went about the mop-up operation. He tidied the stump, bound it.

The rushes flickered out in anticlimax. Later, the production crew would tie up the program with interviews of the family, perhaps a shot of the funeral, a few observations on the problem of gangrene in the aged. Those things were the extras. What counted, what the viewers wanted, was the sheer nastiness of vicarious pain, and that they got in full measure. It was a gladiatorial contest without the gladiators, masochism concealed as medicine. It worked. It pulled in the viewers by the millions.

Northrop patted sweat from his forehead.

"Looks like we got ourselves quite a little show here, boys," he said in satisfaction.

☆

The mood of satisfaction was still on him as he left the building that day. All day he had worked hard, getting the show into its final shape, cutting and polishing. He enjoyed the element of craftsmanship. It helped him to forget some of the sordidness of the program.

Night had fallen when he left. He stepped out of the main entrance and a figure strode forward, a bulky figure, medium height, tired face. A hand reached out, thrusting him roughly back into the lobby of the building.

At first Northrop didn't recognize the face of the man. It was a blank face, a nothing face, a middle-aged empty face.

Then he placed it.

Harry Gardner. The son of the dead man.

"Murderer!" Gardner shrilled. "You killed him! He would have lived if you'd used anesthetics! You phony, you murdered him so people would have thrills on television!"

Northrop glanced up the lobby. Someone was coming around the bend. Northrop felt calm. He could stare this nobody down until he fled in fear.

"Listen," Northrop said, "we did the best medical science can do for your father. We gave him the ultimate in scientific care. We—"

"You murdered him!"

"No," Northrop said, and then he said no more, because he saw the sudden flicker of a slice-gun in the blank-faced man's fat hand. He backed away, but it didn't help, because Gardner punched the trigger and an incandescent bolt flared out and sliced across Northrop's belly just as efficiently as the surgeon's scalpel had cut through the gangrenous leg.

Gardner raced away, feet clattering on the marble floor. Northrop dropped, clutching himself. His suit was seared, and there was a slash through his abdomen, a burn an eighth of an inch wide and perhaps four inches deep, cutting through intestines, through organs, through flesh. The pain hadn't begun yet. His nerves weren't getting the message through to his stunned brain. But then they were, and Northrop coiled and twisted in agony that was anything but vicarious now.

Footsteps approached.

"Jeez," a voice said.

Northrop forced an eye open. Maurillo. Of all people, Maurillo.

"A doctor," Northrop wheezed. "Fast! Christ, the pain! Help me, Ted!"

Maurillo looked down, and smiled.

18

Genesis Project, Andrew Stewart

Without a word, he stepped to the telephone booth six feet away, dropped in a token, punched out a call.

"Get a van over here, fast. I've got a subject, chief."

Northrop writhed in torment. Maurillo crouched next to him. "A doctor," Northrop murmured. "A needle, at least. Gimme a needle! The pain—"

"You want me to kill the pain?" Maurillo laughed. "Nothing doing, chief. You just hang on. You stay alive till we get that hat on your head and tape the whole thing."

"But you don't work for me—you're off the program—"

"Sure," Maurillo said. "I'm with Transcontinental now. They're starting a blood-and-guts show too. Only they don't need waivers."

Northrop gaped. Transcontinental? That bootleg outfit that peddled tapes in Afghanistan and Mexico and Ghana and God knew where else? Not even a network show, he thought. No fee. Dying in agony for the benefit of a bunch of lousy tapeleggers. That was the worst part, Northrop thought. Only Maurillo would pull a deal like that.

"A needle! For God's sake, Maurillo, a needle!"

"Nothing doing, chief. The van'll be here any minute. They'll sew you up, and we'll tape it nice."

Northrop closed his eyes. He felt the coiling intestines blazing within him. He willed himself to die, to cheat Maurillo and his bunch of ghouls. But it was no use. He remained alive and suffering.

He lived for an hour. That was plenty of time to tape his dying agonies. The last thought he had was that it was a damned shame he couldn't star on his own show.

Concentrate 3 Michael Butterworth

SPACE IS COMMUNICATION. To a human being space is realisation. No imagination could. But the awareness of himself on a planet in the universe is psychedelic.

Matter measures time. Having experienced the highways of space and seen the stars and below him the planet Earth…?

The Astronaut

Oceans of scrambled knowledge are in his head—they form a conflict between awareness and balance. Space scrambles his mind.

His suit protects him from the real cold and the real vacuum. But his confused mind (accustomed to a keen perception of space/time) flips.

Space became claustrophobic—suddenly there was no space, no time.…

"Get his hat off."

The struggling body was brought through the hatch into the station boarding bay. An attendant wearing a white gown removed the casualty's headpiece.

His head became hot and buzzed.

"The stars …"

He tried to say there was nothing but the stars
    crawling over his face, as though he found himself
    suddenly drowning in space.

"You became disorientated. All this talk
    about 'highways of space' and 'connections' …"

"No! There were unknown trillions.…"

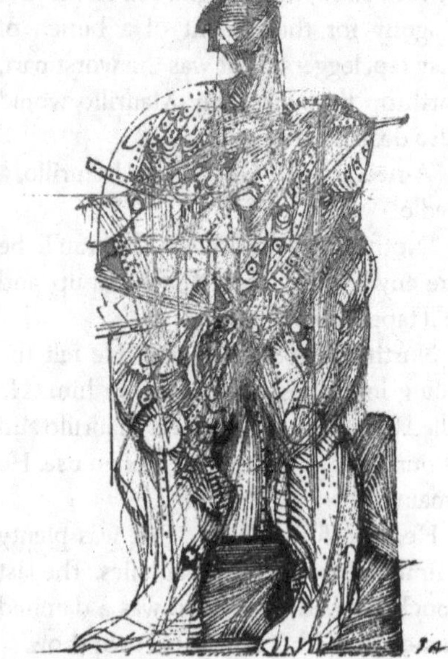

Astronauta, Paulo Sayeg

Valve

avenues of space of
spiralling currents
of low pressure ran
within the vacuum

fields of gravity
wakes of magnetic
debris called the hip
astronaut into line

his mind was filled up
with the works of man

he was a technical
part of the capsule

one country's gain of
name over another's

they led his frail
pressurised head into
the regions of low
pressure
and emptied it

Premium Resurrection Pack – $99

Renan Bernardo

PREMIUM RESURRECTION PACK (Full Mind Backup and Body Upload Included)® for $99. No ads, no separate module purchases.

Sure, Ronnie went to the movies every weekend, drank his share of good wine and occasionally indulged in half-century-old Scotch. But a hundred bucks was too much for a product from CloudMind Enterprises, a company filled with youngsters who had barely made it out of high school.

"Are you sure you don't want the full version, sir?" asked the salesbot in the augmentation store.

"Free is all I need," he said, before the salesbot could babble its default wheedling.

So he bought the Resurrection Pack (Full Mind Backup and Body Upload Included)®. He liked to think he exchanged the word "Premium" for a few ignorable ads and the safety of his $99, which he instead spent on two bottles of Malbec. He was no fool. That was the right place for his money.

At home, he put on the input cap to back up all his valuable thoughts to the cloud server of CloudMind Enterprises. After it was all set up and ready to start, he opened one of the Malbecs to celebrate his thrift.

When the holo-projected progress bar chimed complete, taking a drive to visit

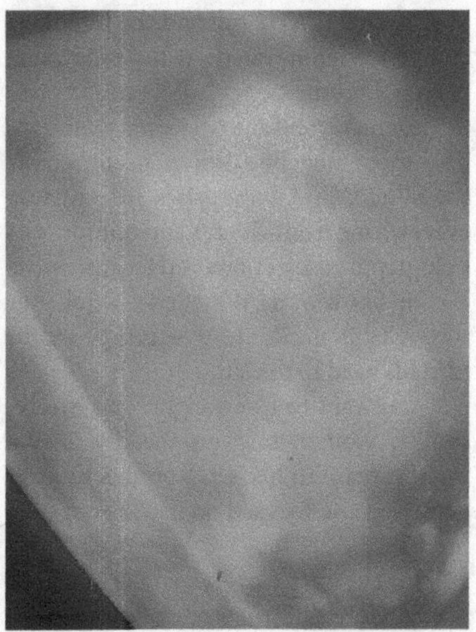

The Spirits of Route 66, No. 27, Dave Vescio

his ex-wife at two in the morning seemed like a good idea. Why not?

Ronnie never saw the garbage truck.

☆

What a sight! Ronnie had never imagined death would be so pleasant. He posed and grinned at his reflection. He didn't have bulging muscles but neither did he have crooked teeth. His face wasn't free of wrinkles, but hair didn't find a lair inside his ears. Happy ending!

Four years had passed since the accident. According to CloudMind, it was the time they needed to develop their bio-replacement bodies.

Ronnie's bank account had been reactivated, inflation-adjusted, and a CloudMind-owned house had been assigned to him. All the recommended procedures for how to reintroduce himself to friends and family and how to reenter the labor market were things he would leave for another week. For a month or two, Ronnie intended to enjoy a post-death vacation. With copious amounts of wine, of course.

The streets were full and the buildings completely renovated with renewable energy production, automatic waste management, and auto-cleaning windows. The most boggling thing, though, was the CloudMind Enterprises logo. It was everywhere, from TV ads and outdoors to holographic projections and toast stamps.

On his way to WineStyle, a jolt ran through his neck. He was compelled to turn his head to the left.

"You want to lose weight?" an overly-smiling woman said on the TV inside the showcase to his left. Ronnie's hearing amplified and focused on it. "Try our new products."

No. He wasn't overweight. He hadn't been before, and he surely wasn't now. But he couldn't take his eyes off the TV. He tried to look just a little bit to the side, but his pupils were automatically pulled to the weight loss product and everything around it blurred.

The commercial ended. Ronnie's head eased up and his sight cleared up.

"The ads," he said it out loud to himself. "But I thought—"

No way. It should've been ads on his phone and tablet....

Bells pealed at WineStyle's door as he entered.

"I want five of those." He pointed at a rack. Two wouldn't do anymore. He needed more, to think about the ads. The salesbot opened its hand, and he pressed his thumb on its palm. A red light flashed on its wrist.

"Sorry, sir. You don't have the module to purchase alcohol."

"What the hell does that mean?"

Oh, but he knew. His new life was freemium.

"I should've paid the $99." He snickered with clenched teeth and snatched up his outdated smartphone to check CloudMind's status. "The full version for people who have already used the system costs ... $99,999?"

"Sir, you can buy the module," said the salesbot.

He touched his smartphone and saw it. Three-Month Alcohol Pack® – $19. He purchased it and left with five bottles of Pinot Noir.

But once at home, he couldn't focus on the TV. West Korea's nuclear crisis and the new wall across the Canadian border seemed like small issues when compared to his condition. He'd already died, his body had been crushed by garbage, and now he had to live like an ad-consumer machine. Ok, he had his second chance in life, but it wasn't working properly.

He had a right to the service warranty.

Ronnie started his old car intent to drive to CloudMind headquarters but almost veered off through his neighbour's front garden.

Oh, yeah. Another $19 gone for the Three-Month Driving Pack (License Does Not Include Parking)®.

Before he could even reach CloudMind, he'd already spent $280 in Three-Month Parking Skills (License Does Not Include Tight Spaces)®, Six-Month Shoelace Tying®, and Lifetime Basic Math®. And the worst of it all? He couldn't purchase new abilities like One-Year French Speaking® and Seven-Month Swimming (Stamina Pack Sold Separately)®. He could only unlock what he knew in his ugly-bodied incarnation.

He lurched inside CloudMind's head-quarters.

"I demand the full version!" Ronnie yelled. Suited people glared at the weirdo. By the looks on their faces, he wasn't the first. "You're stealing my money."

"Sir, relax! The full version is always available." A woman stood in front of him, an unfading smile engraved on her face.

Her tag read, Mrs. Acker—Dissatisfaction PR.

"Selling my soul maybe."

"Sir, you accepted our terms of service when you acquired the free version." The smile persisted.

"This can't be legal." Ronnie clenched his teeth. "Give me the full version or I'll sue you."

Mrs. Acker sighed, her smile fading. "Okay, sir. Would you mind if I switch you to another version? Ad-free. No need for modules."

"Well, yes!" He opened his arms.

Mrs. Acker touched a gleaming icon on her bio-tattooed wrist and indicated his smartphone with her chin. "Read the terms and accept them."

Ronnie stared at his phone for two seconds and tapped Accept.

"Sir …" Mrs. Acker said, rolling her eyes. "Never mind." She turned her back and left.

"Was that hard?" he yelled at her before she entered her office. "Thank you for understanding my rights."

Ronnie left, smiling. He was no fool.

"CloudMind Enterprises is the future," said a bot in an outdoor announcement. "Your future. Our future. With our services, the worldwide economy has grown 287%."

☆

"I want ten of those." Ronnie pointed at the rack in WineStyle. The salesbot opened its palm for the payment.

Before he could reach it with his thumb, a jolt ran through his neck. His sight blurred.

A voice in his head said, "CloudMind Enterprises thanks you for using our services."

He fell hard on the floor.

Ronnie never saw the end date of his Trial Resurrection Pack (Valid Only For Seven Days)®.

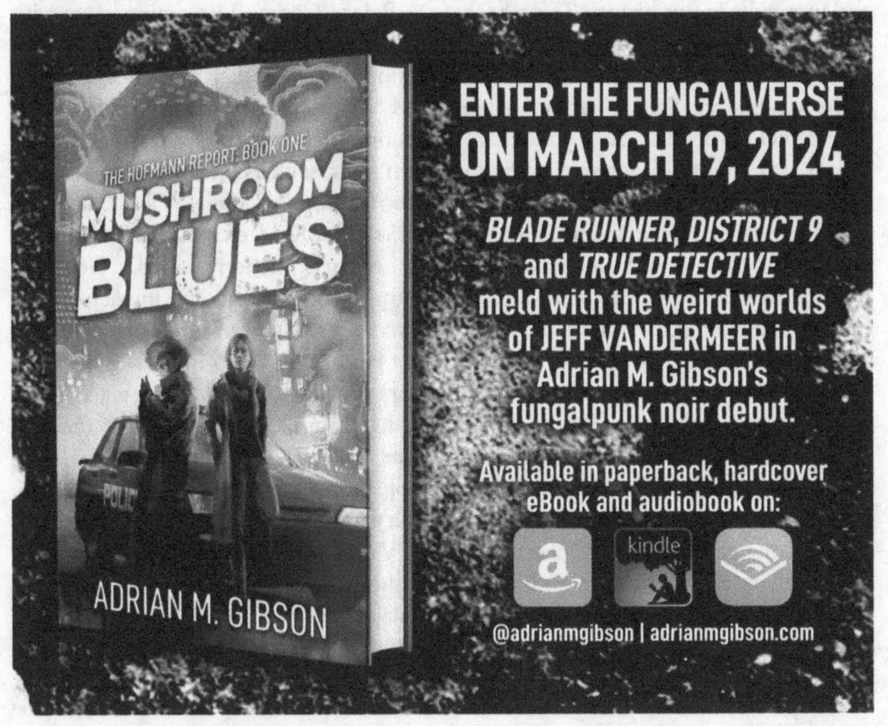

Like Peanut Butter and Jelly: Sports and Science Fiction

Kwame Cavil

It was the summer of 1987. I remember that year in time like it was yesterday. I was nine years old about to turn ten. The world was just starting to become clearly apparent to a young boy. I was no different than any adolescent boy. Girls, school, emotions, sports, food, cars, the dawn of video games, arcades, Michael Jackson and his iconic *Thriller* album were the influencers at that time. I could go on and on about the pop-culture moments in history that were formulated during the '80s era. My whole moral compass was based off the fact that I was a '70s baby that was raised in the '80s. Those eras exposed me to some of the most influential people and moments in our history. This was the era that first introduced me to one of the most (if not the most) influential movies of its generation, *Star Wars*. I'm talking science fiction people!! As a young lad, I always had an affinity for science fiction and sports. In all fairness, what adolescent boy doesn't like the two genres of science and sports? Would we have video games if science fiction didn't inspire the creators of Atari and Nintendo? I think not.

Seamlessly, the two genres of sports and science always seem to collide or coincide with each other. From learning how plants grow in the garden in your front yard, to trampling those plants from playing football and getting tackled in that same garden. I still remember my Mom yelling at my brothers and me for being too rough and close to her precious garden. From taking your telescope out and looking through the lens into space (if you were fortunate to have one), to watching the shuttle actually go into space from its launch pad at NASA. Or watching Michael Jordan look like he was launching himself into space with his famous free throw line slam dunk, I've been hooked on science fiction and sports. I know there are some kids out there that may not have the passion I had as a young boy for science and sports but science fiction is what made me dare to dream. Sports allowed me to reach those dreams. We have to dream first before we can achieve those dreams. Thanks to education, the expectations placed on me by my parents and family, and heroes I idolized, I could look to the stars and dare to be great.

Before George Lucas blessed us with his pop cultural masterpiece of science fiction, we had other examples of Space and the infinite possibilities of science fiction. There were other classics in their own right, such as *E.T., War of the Worlds, Star Trek, Space Odyssey, Close Encounters of the Third Kind,* etc., that helped inspire us science fiction nerds. However, nothing compares to the impact of *Star Wars* to a generation of teenagers during that period. By 1987, the first three Stars Wars movies (or the last three according to the chronological timeline of the *Star Wars* trilogy) had moved into living room homes and out of the big screen. Everybody who had a VHS or VCR, and a TV could have the "Force" be with them or choose the "dark side" in the confines of their own homes. I can vividly remember having a flashlight and pretending to have a "green" lightsaber, while making the famous sound of that lightsaber. It's hard for me to pinpoint what grabbed my attention first about the iconic series. The very thought of the unknown and the "what if" of science fiction ultimately drew my attention.

The underlying storyline of good vs. evil being depicted through its fictional equivalent of the "Force" vs. the "dark side" could be a determining factor in my love for Star Wars. Star Wars and other science fictional movies alike were impactful on my sports career. I wanted to be a hero like Luke Skywalker. The "Force" to me was equivalent to an athlete being in the "zone." There were times where I witnessed my favorite athlete get into the "zone." A phenomenon known to athletes where their preparation meets opportunity and a real-life "out of body" experience occurs in the moment. For example, when Kobe Bryant or Michael Jordan would have these scoring bursts in a single game, they often referred to themselves as feeling like they were in the "zone." This mental zone can be only achieved through alignment of the mind, body, and soul. This mental mastery allows athletes to tap into a source only few can achieve through hard work, dedication, and determination (Kobe's iconic 81 points in a single game or Jordan's 69 points in the Boston Garden). Being in the "zone" and the "Force" parallel each other because of the mental prowess it takes to achieve this mental state. Every now and then, a person can achieve this mental mastery that connects with the body and causes them to be in a "zone" that they can't even explain at times. Sounds like the "Force" to me. Oftentimes I've called myself a "Jedi" in football. Let me explain. After years and years of practice an athlete will achieve a mastery level that prepares them for a moment in the "zone." It's

a feeling that can only be compared to having the "Force" in that moment.

Sports can play an integral part in a young person's life. There are so many life lessons that can be learned through sports. Integrity, honesty, hard work, and dedication are some of the lessons I learned from playing sports. Science fiction is a genre where a young person gets to create and explore. Science fiction allows people to dream and wonder the infinite possibilities. You can be whatever you want or create whomever you like. I think science fiction continues to make an appearance in sports. I've witnessed sports programming use it in their depiction of sports and its athletes to viewers. They often refer to athletes and their feats as

'80s SF, Richard Grieco

fictional characters or characteristics. It's in their nicknames: Michael "Air" Jordan, Kobe "Black Mamba" Bryant, Shawn "Matrix" Marion, Dave "Cobra" Parker. These nicknames were given to them because of the athletic prowess that often resembled what they were being named for. Even I had a nickname because of how I glided across the field. Announcers would call me "Cadillac" Cavil because of the comparison to the smooth ride you could achieve from riding in a Cadillac.

In conclusion, sports and science fiction are intertwined like peanut butter and jelly. You can enjoy them separately, but together they are out of this world.

Contact

"Why are your life bearers
not your prime decisioners?"
The BelovedBeloved asked us
"Where are you are priestessmages,
your doctorseers, your doulasages?"

They were speaking our language
and struggling with our flat cultures.
Why were we made sterile for this voyage?
Couldn't we hold our fertilized eggs
until ready to grow and birth? Couldn't our
empty men assist with the carrying?

It takes the BBs more than an earth year
like African elephants and the sperm whales
they resemble, fluid filled, square heads,
resonant with light, radiant with understanding
redolent with psychotropic scent, actuating aromas,
to cocreate their supple, ready, glistening young.

They struggled with our simple, reductive, linearity
being polite, exceedingly it seemed, perhaps trying
to hide their shock and possible faint revulsion
speaking as simply, as slowly, as they could

paring down the bundled constructs
of their multivariate consciousness
accommodating the profound disabilities
of our youth and our stunning uncompassion

Abdução, Paulo Sayeg

—Akua Lezli Hope

The Horn

Zdravka Evtimova

YOUP HAD DECIDED to let himself go, all the way. He had spent last night with a blonde again and had not even bothered to remember her name. She had told him she had died and been regenerated seven times, and Youp had pretended to believe her, but the superficial black stripes on her shoulders and head, when you parted her hair, told a different story. Especially the ones on her head. They were so close together they gave him chills up and down his spine—she must have been in the regenerating rooms at least a dozen times, probably in the "deluxe" accommodations, the treatment followed by a lavish and costly procedure—the colour of her skin summoned thoughts of fabulously expensive balm. Youp had erased her face from his videotheque, but he was still in the throes of last night's excitement, so he decided to indulge himself with another blonde tonight. He knew that pleasures of this sort cost approximately three times his salary, but he was sure he would fail the physical exam this month and then would be forced into the standard regenerating rooms. The treatment left such deep and visible dark grey lines all over the body that afterwards one looked like a quilt sewn together from differently coloured rags and bits of fabric. He considered himself born under a lucky star, because the computer for initiating intimate contacts had paired him with such a charming creature—flaxen-haired, with green eyes that moved about in a distracted way, and an appearance that, at first glance, revealed no signs of her ever-having set foot in a standard regenerating room. Impatient, Youp wanted to proceed to the dark hotel room, for which he had paid a fat bundle, but when the woman said a few words he felt goosebumps up and down his back and slowed his steps.

"You know, death looks quite becoming on you, dummy. Don't try to fight it! Don't try to hide the lines on your skin! They give a fierce expression to your face. You know, I sometimes envy those who go through the standard procedure."

Youp hesitated. He could get rid of her—the woman was obviously crazy. But after a moment's thought he remembered that the computer for initiating intimate contacts had already charged him for the room, so he decided against it. The blonde woman had already started to caress him, and that switched on a pleasant sensation. "Crazy or not, at least she does it well," he thought. "Besides, I'll never see her again." Actually, the rules for intimate contacts did allow partners to meet repeatedly, but no one ever did. It would have been much too boring. The woman went on with her chatter.

"Just imagine, dummy. Sometimes I spend a whole six months without having to use the regenerating rooms."

Though he was generally regarded as a stable, well-composed person who could control himself, Youp trembled visibly. This one was definitely off her rocker. Not that all the ones he had met before had been sane. Actually, Seva, the only woman whose name he could remember and about whom he kept inquiring among his colleagues, was also mad. So mad, in fact, that he couldn't think about her without ending up dead drunk, thus using up his next two or three paychecks before he had even received them. Seva—an unusual name. When he had heard it for the first time he had made fun of it. He knew he would never see her again.

"Six months and not a single viral infection in my blood! No rheumatism, no diabetes, nothing. I'm completely healthy."

Youp decided to ignore her rambling and babbling. He knew for a fact that it was impossible to survive on earth for more than a month without resorting to the regenerating rooms. The atmosphere was so filled with poisons and toxins that your lungs fell apart in forty days. Contact with the soil turned your skin into dust within a week. Water discoloured and decomposed your blood in a month or so, provided you drank it in small doses. At least that's what he had been told; he himself had never stayed away from the regenerating room for more than fifteen days.

"Six months without regeneration!" He grunted, trying to humour her. "Where do you work, honey?"

"At the Resurrection Laboratory," she chimed in. "Everything there is so sterile, so boring, that—"

Youp whistled. "The Resurrection Laboratory!" Some of the people who worked there could be quite refined.... But sometimes they felt drawn to brutal, primitive characters, and put their numbers in a regular computer for initiating intimate contacts. But who cared? People got tired of always being among the elite. Youp had chanced upon just such a woman. Maybe he could ask her. He was wary. Still, he could ask… It was too soon, though. Perhaps a little later. Youp swore under his breath. The week after they dragged Seva away in a police van, he and two colleagues had tried to die permanently. Naturally, they had been regenerated once more and sent back to work. Society needed their golden hands, their invaluable experience—that's what the television commentator had said.

Omulu do Brasil, Paulo Sayeg

Youp had even received a pay raise. Still, he had little tolerance for this society, this horde of dreary characters who had been regenerated a million times. Sometimes he wished he would never be resurrected again, would never have to go back to his dingy office and dreary job as a wholesale distributor of soap and cosmetics. But there was nothing he could do about it. It was much cheaper to regenerate the sickly and diseased and let them loose on the hazards of life fit and healthy than it was to purify the sludge-like soil or the brownish muck they called water by force of habit. The need to have children born had disappeared, and so had the need to squander money on hospitals, schools, kindergartens and nursery schools. People came back regenerated, their experience intact, their health fully restored, bragging about this disease or that they had had earlier but had been cured of. And so on until the next dying time. Women didn't lose their sexual savvy—like this doll here. She was okay.

Real death simply ceased to exist. And yet Youp hated his job as a wholesale soap distributor with a passion.

"You know, dummy," blurted the blonde excitedly, "once they nearly threw me out of the laboratory. Do you know why?"

"Why?" Youp echoed listlessly.

"I absentmindedly left a patient's blood plasma out in the sun. You have no idea what happened to this man after we regenerated him! The poor idiot had a horn growing right out of his chest! He went berserk—he gutted the chief surgeon, ripped open the faces of a couple of nurses … What excitement! Naturally, we had to regenerate all of them."

Youp felt himself getting tense. He licked his lips with a gravelly tongue. His blood pounded away in his temples.

"And what ever happened to that character, the one with the horn?"

"We had to liquidate him, of course," laughed the blonde.

"And then you ran him through the regenerators again?"

"Absolutely not! We liquidated him forever."

Youp let out a groan. The blonde kissed him and resumed her benumbing prattle. But he was thinking of Seva—that mad woman. "I want a child," she had said to Youp. "A real child. Mine and yours. I'll take care of it. Please, hide me somewhere. At your place." At first Youp had said no. Then he thought, "Why not?" and had taken Seva to his squalid living quarters. At least that way they would not withhold money from his sex account until the police inspectors found her. And then the child was born. At first Youp thought he would kill it himself; he had never heard of a child being born and couldn't even start guessing what kind of fine they would impose on him for it. He had hidden Seva and taken her through the regenerating rooms illegally. This was going to cost him a fine of a quarter of a million! He had to get rid both of Seva and the baby. But he couldn't do it; from the moment the boy was born everything had changed. He would hurry like mad to get home. He would lean over his old clothes where the little one lie cuddled. He would pay outrageous sums of money for clean, filtered water. Eventually, however, the police had found Seva. Youp couldn't find out who had betrayed him; probably some friend who sincerely felt for him and wanted to spare him the disgrace and the huge fine.

"My colleagues will never believe that I came into contact with a person like you," said Youp.

The blonde laughed. "Take this," she said, thrusting a bundle of cash into his hand. "Now they will believe you."

"The word was going around that you had regenerated some baby in your laboratory," Youp ventured. The blonde tensed up nervously in his grasp, so he added quickly, "maybe we shouldn't talk of such things?"

"No, we shouldn't," the woman smiled, calming down. "Apparently, some perverse character had wanted something stupid like that around. The woman with the baby refused to give his name."

Seva! It dawned on him like a huge submarine suddenly emerging from the depths of the ocean. Seva. She had not betrayed him. Of course she hadn't. If she had told on him they would have sent him to Seycard; there the regenerating rooms were set up so that when you came out your eyes popped out and glazed over, and you went mute. But there is even a use for idiots; doctors have to have material to experiment on, after all. So Seva had not betrayed him. Mad, stark raving mad. She could have accused him of rape and coercion—but she hadn't. He had promised his annual salary as a reward for any information on her. Maybe someone had run into her in some intimate contact…. Yet no one had ever responded. He was going crazy with fear that they had sent her to Seycard, so he signed on as a volunteer to go and repair the facilities there, but he didn't find her. The thought of her being with someone else drove him insane with jealousy. But at least that was preferable to knowing with certainty that they had not regenerated her, that she had disappeared from the face of the earth. "Seva. My dear …"

"What?!" the blonde shrieked in delight. "'My dear?' Is that what you just called me? You're incredible, sweetie."

"Dear?" Where had he picked up the word? No one had used it in years. Seva. Seva. Seva….

"Did you really regenerate that baby?" Youp threw in gingerly.

"Why in the world would we do that? No, we left it to its own end."

"To its end? To … die?" he froze with fear at the sound of the word. "To die forever?"

"Of course, dummy." The blonde woman smiled and started stroking his hair. "Both the baby and his hare-brained mother, who, come to think of it, wasn't bad-looking at all. Will anybody believe that you called me 'My dear?' I really liked it, though it did sound kind of loony, didn't it?"

If only he had tried to stop the paramedics when they took the baby away! Youp hadn't shown his face at all. That would have meant regeneration at Seycard for sure. He remembered how the day before he had taken the little one's fingers and put them to his own cheek. Loony, true, but nice. It had felt so nice! Somehow he had hoped that at some point in his life he would see a boy and say to himself, "That's my boy." He had hoped, yet … But they would see! He would show them!

Maybe it would have been better if Seva had betrayed him back then.

"They'll see, all of them!" he kept repeating after the blonde beauty had departed. His joints hurt, his heart had been rattling irregularly for quite some time. He was definitely due for another regeneration. As usual Youp prepared his blood plasma carefully. But this time, contrary to all instructions, he left the transparent container out in the sun for more than an hour. "They'll see, Seva!" Youp hated his job at the soap office more than ever before.

His first impulse when he emerged from the next dying and regeneration routine was to reach out and feel his chest. "Seva, my dear!" he whispered. Those forgotten, silly words. In the middle of his chest cavity his shaking fingers touched a crusty, sharp-edged protrusion.

It was a huge, heavy horn.

Book Feature

UFOs: Generals, Pilots, and Government Officials Go on the Record

courtesy of
Leslie Kean

AN AIR FORCE MAJOR is ordered to approach a brilliant UFO in his Phantom jet over Tehran. He repeatedly attempts to engage and fire on unusual objects heading right towards his aircraft, but his missile control is locked and disabled. Witnessed from the ground, this dogfight becomes the subject of a secret report by the U.S. Defense Intelligence Agency.

In Belgium, an Air Force colonel investigates a series of widespread sightings of unidentified triangular objects, and he sends F-16s to attempt a closer look. Many hundreds of eyewitnesses, including on-duty police officers, file reports with a group of scientists working in conjunction with the Air Force.

Here at home, a retired chief of the FAA's Accidents and Investigations Division reveals the agency's response to a thirty-minute encounter between an aircraft and a gigantic UFO over Alaska, documented on radar, which occurred during his watch.

All three of these distinguished men have written breathtaking, firsthand accounts about these extraordinary incidents for Leslie Kean's acclaimed New York Times bestseller *UFOs: Generals, Pilots, and Government Officials Go on the Record.* They are joined by Air Force generals and a host of high-level sources—including Fife Symington III, former governor of Arizona and Nick Pope, former head of the British Defence Ministry's UFO Investigative Unit— who agreed to write their own detailed, personal chapters about UFO encounters and investigations, for the first time.

Kean, an independent investigative reporter, spent over ten years studying the still unexplained UFO phenomenon and publishing articles on the topic in mainstream media. She reviewed hundreds of government documents, aviation reports, radar data, and case studies with corroborating physical evidence, and carefully examined scientifically analyzed photographs. She also interviewed dozens of high-level officials and aviation witnesses from around the world. Kean draws on her research to separate fact from fiction and to lift the veil on decades of U.S. government misinformation.

We know that of all UFO sightings reported, 90 to 95 percent can be explained as ordinary phenomena. However, within that remaining small percentage, spectacular well-documented UFO events have been officially investigated by government agencies around the world, yet no conventional explanations were found. Throughout her book, Kean presents irrefutable evidence that unknown flying objects—metallic, luminous, and seemingly able to maneuver in ways that defy the laws of physics—actually exist.

No one yet knows what these objects are, even though they affect aviation safety and possibly national security. The phenomenon has been officially acknowledged by numerous foreign governments. For these reasons and many others, Kean concludes that the UFO problem must be more widely recognized and ultimately solved through an unbiased scientific investigation. The material presented throughout this landmark book is sobering, unflinching, and undeniably awe-inspiring, and moves us towards a goal of properly addressing this worldwide mystery.

I Hope I Call You Back

Tara Campbell

I.

HELLO, YOU'VE REACHED ALISON. Please leave a message and I'll call you back.

II.

Hello, you've reached Alison. Leave a message and I'll call you back, but please also be aware that I'm about to go in for stress reduction surgery, so I may not— call you back.

III.

Hello, it's Alison. Please be aware, I've just had stress reduction brain surgery that has made it impossible for me to hear people who have created too much— well, stress—in my life. This means I might listen to a message and hear absolutely nothing; I won't even know you've called. So, excuse me in advance if I don't call back.

IV.

Hi, Alison here. I had stress reduction brain surgery last week, so I might not hear your message. I've opted for the involuntary option: the system automatically analyzes micro-changes in pulse and respiration while screening my memories of the person who's calling. I don't have to make a conscious choice—the system does it for me, erasing not only the content of the message from my mind, but also any memory of who was assessed. When I finish checking messages, I'll know that someone has been filtered out, but not who, and the process repeats itself, no matter how many times I listen. So, if I don't call back, please know it's not on purpose. I mean, it's not me making the choice, it's my brain.

V.

Hello, you've reached Alison. I may not call you back because I may not even know you've called, you know, with my surgery and all. It cost extra, this guilt-free option, but it was worth it not to have to make the decision myself. Although, in a way, I suppose I am making the decision, by which I mean my body is making the decision, without interference from pressures related to personal guilt or social norms. When you think about it, it's the purest, healthiest form of decision-making there is—your body is the ultimate arbiter, able to weed out destructive elements, ridding itself of toxins.

You may wonder what happens if it weeds out important people, like my mother, for example. Maybe you are, in fact, my mother, about to leave a message—maybe again? Maybe you'll leave one and get screened out, although I would be surprised if that happened to you, Mom. But it could happen, I suppose, on a purely cellular level. Childhood memories and all that. I mean, adolescence, right? Hopes. Expectations. It's almost impossible that there would be a complete absence of stress with parents. But then, if the system were that sensitive, really, would any parents talk to any children anymore? Would any family talk at all? Leave a message and find out.

VI.

Hi, it's Alison, and let me just apologize right away in case your message gets stress-filtered out, even if I consider you dearest family or friend—because doesn't closeness naturally entail emotional entanglement? This is exactly why the system is so expensive. It's highly scientific, with a battery of tests to calibrate the levels of stress the subject is willing to endure, coupled with an analysis of how much stress can reasonably be tolerated to preserve societal cohesion. Of course, some of the questions they asked were a little strange. I don't know how they interpreted the part about my fourteenth birthday party, for example, or the fact that I don't remember being dropped off at kindergarten. I mean, what does that mean? What were they writing down when I said that?

VII.

Hi, there. It's been about six months since my brain surgery, so if I call you back, it means you got through the stress reduction filter. If I don't, please know that it's not because I don't want to call you back, but because the surgery is working. It's just a biological fact at this point, given my physiological response to someone that would be—is? Has been? Still is?—would be toxic for me to hear from. I have no idea who you are, though: when I play back a message, I literally don't hear anything. Dead air, with no memory of what I heard and filtered out. I suppose it's doing its trick. Except …

Except, sometimes I wonder who's being filtered out of my life when I sit here, listening for someone's voice and hearing only silence, trying to guess who was on the other end and whether they suspected they'd be on the chopping block, their words essentially disappearing into smoke as soon as they left their mouths. Maybe you've already hung up; or maybe you're simply sitting on the other end of the line, wondering what to say, composing a message you're afraid I might not—maybe even know gut-deep I won't—ever receive.

Still, I hope you try.

VIII.

Hey, it's Alison. It's coming up on a year since I got my stress-reduction brain surgery, and I'm not even sure why I'm re-recording this outgoing message, because I'm probably not even going to listen to messages at all anymore because I can't stop wondering who I'm not hearing this time, and whether this is your first time trying to reach me, or if you've called again and again and again. And after I listen to all the silence, I hang up and think, *I haven't heard from so-and-so in a while*, and I wonder if that's you who just tried to call, or if they haven't reached out at all. And it's led me to wonder if forgetting you—whoever you are—is more stressful than hearing you in the first place. So, whoever's out there, please know, even if I never call you back, I'm glad you called. And yes, I will keep on listening, because I've actually been able to hear some of you again, faintly, and I'm trying to hear more of you—whoever you are—each day.

IX.

Hello, it's Alison. Thanks for calling. It's the first anniversary of my stress reduction brain surgery, and I'm able to hear much more now. Turns out the system isn't the only one in charge: the more toxicity I filter *myself*, the more the good gets through. So please give me a try—whether I hear your voice or not, I'll try to call you back. And if it takes me a while to call you, please forgive me and pick up. Please stay on the line, even if I start answering questions you didn't ask, or responding to something you didn't say, please stay on the line. If I say something that makes no sense, it's only because I can't hear you talking—yet. It's just me trying to reconnect. Please know, I'm listening to you, and learning to hear you better, even if I can't hear a word you say.

Please leave a message.

It Must Be Art : Big O Poster Artists of the 1960s and 70s
Michael Fishel and Nigel Suckling

Throughout the 1960s and 70s, London-based Big O Posters helped define the new and democratic art medium of the psychedelic poster, a vehicle for rebellion against the old order that went hand in hand with the music, literature, and film of the time. This is a comprehensive collection of works published by Big O artists, astonishingly creative folks whose artistry developed almost completely outside the influence of the art establishment. Included in more than 300 images are works by 19 artists, including Martin Sharp, Roger Dean H.R. Giger, Robert Venosa, and Vali Myers, whose signature styles include sci-fi, fantasy, visionary, botanical, and surrealism. In addition to hundreds of original works, this book digs below the surface to offer insights and anecdotes about the era, the artistic process, and reveal connections to artists from the past (Aubrey Beardsley, Alphonse Mucha, Kay Nielsen) whose spirit chimed with the age of Big O Posters.

Size: 8.5in x 11.0in | Pages: 304 | 300+ colour & b/w images
Binding: Hardback | Publisher: Schiffer Books
ISBN: 9780764355486
PRICE: $50.00

Ship in a Bottle, Anchored

You are a ship in a bottle, glass cracked,
sand swallowing like mud, wood rotten,
moth chewed, and when the sea's tendrils
enter the lips of the bottle held in its silent
echo, there is nowhere for you to float
because here the sky is not endless, here
the water can only enter with nowhere
to leave, here the sand only rises and churns
and blinds rather than sinking, settling,
to create a bed, a foundation for the land
on which you desired to dig your fingers
into, wooden planks you wanted to tear
from your body when you arrived, laying
them down atop the green, the soil, the trees,
the rivers that were already there. You
wanted to rip the sails from their anchors
and use them as flags. You wanted to detach
the wheel and use it as a shepherd for those
who do not wish to follow. You desired to take
your compass and gouge room in the heart
chambers of every living thing and plant
the needle within yourself so you are
the true North anyone could ever know—
now.
And so, you chip away at the bottle's glass,
thinking of your dream as the glass fractures,
splinters, cracks, then shatters to unleash you
into a world that desperately wanted you trapped.
For them, your return isn't triumph, your return
isn't glorious, you are not their saviour. Your
return means that they will have to create
bottles of their own. And as you try to shatter
their new shield, you might think they, like you,
saw it as prison, but really, they saw it as a haven
against you. And to you, there is no difference
between bottle or battle, but to them,
it is the difference between answering
the sea's rage and remaining on dry shores—
unanchored.

—Ai Jiang

Time Junkies

Bodies slumped outside
grungy, crumbling tenements,
brown skin fading into translucence;
molecular degradation,
they're becoming as invisible as they feel
to a failing nation.
Tell me of those times, they say,
we'll have water and clear skies,
shelter and peace and love and …

Searching for a quick fix,
they long for utopias glimpsed,
for futures that have slipped
from their hands like grains of sand.
Cross their palms with silver
before they fade away,
reassure them today
that there'll be no sorrow
tomorrow.
But they already know.
Don't they

—Pedro Iniguez

Chrysalis

David Brin

***Like every person** who ever contemplated existence, I've wondered if the world was made for me—whole and new—this very morning, along with counterfeit memories of what came before.*

Recollection is unreliable, as are the records we inherit each day. Even those we made the night before—our jotted notes or formal reports, our memorials carved deep in stone—even they might have been concocted, along with memories of breakfast, by some deity or demon. Or by an adolescent 28th-century sim-builder, a pimpled devil, playing god.

Find the notion absurd?

Was that response programmed into you?

Come now. History was always written by the victors, while losers passed their entire lives only to be noted as brief speedbumps. And aren't all triumphs weathered by time?

I sound dour. A grumpy grownup. Well, so it goes, when tasked with cleaning messes left by others. Left by my former self.

And so, with a floating sigh of adulthood, I dive into this morass—records, electronic trails and "memories" that float before me like archaic dreams. Ruminations of an earlier, ignorant—not innocent—me.

It all started medically, you see. With good intentions, like so many sins.

☆

January 6, 2029:

Organ replacement. For a generation it was hellishly difficult and an ethical nightmare. Millions lingered anxiously on waiting lists, guiltily hoping that a stranger out there would conveniently crash his car—someone with identical histocompatibility markers, so you might take a kidney or a liver with less probability of rejection. His bad luck transforming into your good fortune. Her death giving you a chance to live.

Even assuming an excellent match, there'd be an agony of immunosuppressant therapy and risk of lethal infections. Nor was it easy on us doctors. When a transplant failed, you felt you were letting two patients down, both recipient and donor.

Sci-fi dystopias warned where this might lead. Sure enough, some countries started scheduling criminal executions around the organ want-list. Granting reprieves till someone important needed a heart … your heart. Then, off to disassembly.

When micro-surgeons got good enough to transplant arms, legs and faces—everything but the squeal—we knew it was only a matter of time till the Niven Scenario played out. Voters would demand capital punishment for more than just heinous crimes. Your fourth speeding ticket? Time to *spread you around.* Is it really death, when nearly all your parts live on, within a hundred of your neighbors?

Hell gaped before us. There had to be a better way.

And we found it! *Grow new parts* in the lab. Pristine, compatible and ethically clean.

☆

Caterpillar eat! Chew that big old leaf.
Ugly little caterpillar, your relief,
When you've chomped your fill, will be to find a stem.
Weave yourself a dressing room, hang in it, and then
Change little caterpillar, grow your wings!
Now go find your destiny. Nature sings.

☆

When we started trying to form organs *in situ,* George Stimson claimed the process would turn out to be simple. He offered me a wager—ten free meals at his favorite salad bar. I refused the bet.

"Those are your stakes? Lunch at the Souplantation? Acres of veggies?"

"Hey, what's wrong with healthy eating? They have the genuine stuff."

OVNIs–UFOs, Paulo Sayeg

"My point exactly, George. Every time we go there, I look at a plate full of greens and think: *this* is what *real* food eats!"

He blinked a couple of times, then chuckled at my carnivorous gibe before swinging back to the main topic—building new human organs.

"Seriously. I bet we can get away with a really simple scaffold. No complicated patterns of growth factors and inhibitors. None of this stuff."

He waved at the complex map of a human esophagus that I had worked out over the weekend—a brilliantly detailed plan to embed a stretchy tube of plastic and collagen with growth and suppression factors. Along with pluripotent cells, of course, the miracle ingredient, cultured from a patient's own tissues. Some of the inserted chemicals would encourage the stems to become epithelial cells *here* and *here*. Others would prompt them to produce cartilage there and muscle-attachment sites *here* and *here* and …

…and George thought my design way too complex.

"Just lace in a vascular system to feed the stems," he said. "They'll do the rest."

"But how will they know which adult cell type to turn into?" I demanded. "Without being told? How will you get these interleaved fans and arrays of connective tissues and tendons and vessels and glands.…"

This was way back near the turn of the century, when we had just figured out how to take skin or gut cells and transform them back into raw stems, a pre-differentiated state that was *pluripotent,* or capable of becoming almost any other variety, from nerves to astrocytes to renal … anything at all! Exciting times. But how to assign those

38

roles in something as complex as a body organ? We had found specific antigens, peptides, growth factors, but so many tissues would only form if they were laid out in ornate patterns. As complex as the organs they were meant to rebuild or replace.

Patterns we were starting to construct! Using the same technology as an ink-jet printer, spray-forming intricate 3-D configurations and hoping someday to replicate the complex vein patterns within a kidney, then a spinal cord, and eventually …

"We won't have to specify in perfect detail," George assured me. "Life will find a way."

I ignored the movie cliché. Heck, why not try his approach in a pig or two?

We started by ripping out a cancer-ridden esophagus, implanting a replacement made of structural polygel and nutrients. This scaffolding we'd lace with the test animal's own stem cells, insert the replacement …

Whereupon, *voilá*. Step back, and witness a miracle! After some trial and error—and much to my astonishment—George proved right. In those first esophagi we implanted—and in subsequent human tests—my fine patterns of specific growth factors proved unnecessary. No need to command them specifically: "*You* become a mucus lining cell, *you* become a support structure…." Somehow, the stems divided, differentiated, divided again, growing into a complete adult esophagus. And they did it *within* the patient!

"How do they know?" I asked, despite expecting in advance what George would say.

"They don't *know*, Beverly. Each cell is reacting only to its surroundings. To chemical messages and cues from its environment, especially its immediate neighbors. And it emits cues to affect *them*, as well. Each one is acting as a perfect—if complicated—little …"

"… cellular automaton. Yes, yes."

Others, watching us finish each other's sentences, would liken us to an affectionate old married couple. Which in several ways we were. Few noticed the undercurrent of scorching rivalry that by now spanned decades. Spectacularly successful teamwork, as far as the world was concerned.

Well, the world was easy to fool. As we both had been, two or three marriages ago, each, back when George was the most handsome, brilliant and *vital* man I ever knew … and when I used to so look forward to looking into a mirror or appearing on *Science Channel* shows. Now? They all still called us brilliant, at least. Though I have also heard *cranky* and *curmudgeonly*….

Well, scientific detachment doesn't mean we're immune to grumpiness over life's inevitable decline. In fact, it stokes an outraged retort: *Who says it's inevitable?!*

George and I still shared a simple cause. To spit death in the eye at every turn.

"So," I continued, "just by jostling against each other in the chemical pattern of the scaffold, that alone is enough for the stem cells to sort themselves out? Differentiating into dozens of types, in just the right geometry?"

"Geometry, yes." George nodded vigorously. "Geometrical biochemistry. I like that. Good. Isn't that how cells sort themselves into vastly complex patterns inside a developing fetal brain? But of course you see what all of this means."

He gestured along a row of lab benches at more recent accomplishments, each carefully tended by one or more students.

—a functioning liver, grown from scaffolding inside a mouse, till we carved it out. The organ now lay *in vitro*, still working, fed by a nearby blood pump—

—a cat whose lower intestines had been replaced by polygel tubing … that was now completely lined with all the right cells: in effect two meters of fully functioning gut—

—two dozen rats with amputated forelegs, whose stumps were encased in gel-capsules. Along simple frameworks, new limbs could be seen taking shape as the creature's own cells (with a little coaxing from my selected scarring inhibitors and stem-sims) migrated to correct positions in a coalescing structure of flesh and linear bone. Lifting my gaze, I saw cages where older creatures hobbled about on regrown appendages. So far, they were clumsy, club-like, footless things. Yet they were astonishing.

And yes, I saw what George *meant*.

"We always assumed that mammals had lost the ability to regenerate organs, because it doesn't happen in nature. Reptiles, amphibians and some fish can regrow whole body parts. But mammals in the wild? They … we … can only do simple damage control, covered by scar tissue."

"But if we *prevent* scarring," he prompted. "If we lay down scaffolds, nutrient webs —"

"—then yes. There emerges a level of self-repair far more sophisticated than we ever imagined possible in mammals." I shook my head. "But it makes no sense! Why retain a general capability when nature never supplies the conditions to use it? These latent repair systems re-emerge only when we provide the right circumstances in our lab."

George pondered a moment. "Beverly, I think you're asking the wrong question. Have you ever wondered: why did mammals lose … or give up … this ability in the first place?"

"Of course I have! The answer is obvious. With our fast metabolisms, we have to eat a lot. No mammal in the wild can afford to lie around for weeks, even months, the way a reptile can, while waiting for a major limb or organ to regrow. He'd starve long before it finished. Better to concentrate on things mammals are good at, like speed, agility and brains, to avoid getting damaged in the first place. Mammalian regeneration probably vanished back in the Triassic, over a hundred million years ago."

He nodded. "Seems a likely explanation. But what's puzzling you—" He prompted me with a lifted eyebrow, a coaxing gesture of encouragement that I used to find charming, almost back in the Triassic.

"What puzzles me is why the capability has been hanging around all this time! Lurking in our genome, never used!"

George held up a hand. "I think we're getting ahead of ourselves. First, let's admit that humans have changed the balance, the equation. We are now mammals who can lie around for weeks or months while others feed us. First the family and tribe took up this duty, back in the Stone Age, then village and town and—"

"—and Canadian National Health, sure. And those innovations increased *survival rates* after serious injuries," I admitted. "But it never resulted in organ or limb *regrowth!*"

Abruptly I realized that half a dozen grad students had lowered their tools and instruments and were sidling closer. They knew this was historic stuff. *Nobel-level* stuff. Heck, I didn't mind them listening in. But shirking shouldn't be blatant! I sure never got away with it, back when I served my time as a lab-slave. My withering glare sent them scurrying back to their posts.

Oblivious, as usual, George simply blathered on. "Yes, yes. For that to happen, for those dormant abilities to re-awaken, it seems we need to fill in all sorts of lost bits and pieces. Parts of the regrowth process that were mislaid across—what's your estimate, again?"

"A hundred million years. Ever since advanced therapsids became fully warm-blooded, early in the age of dinosaurs. That's when major organ regrowth must have gone dormant in our ancestors. Heck, it's not surprising that some of the sub-processes have faded or become flawed. I'm amazed that any of them—apparently *most* of them—are still here at all!"

"Are you complaining?" he asked with an arched eyebrow.

"Of course not. If all of this holds up," I waved around the lab, now quadrupled in size, as major funding sources rushed to support our work, "the therapeutic implications will be staggering. Millions of lives will be saved or improved. No one will have to languish on organ donor waiting lists, praying for someone else to have bad luck."

I didn't mention the other likely benefit. One more year of breakthroughs and the two of us would be shoo-ins for Stockholm. In fact, so certain was that starting to seem, that I had begun dismissing the Nobel from my thoughts! Taking for granted what had—for decades—been a central focus of my life, my existence. It felt queer, but the Prize scarcely mattered to me anymore. I could see it now. A golden disk accompanied by bunches of new headaches. Speeches and advisory panels. Public events and "inspirational" appearances, far more than George would face, because every charismatic woman scientist has to go the rounds, doing *role-model duty for girls*. It would all add up to pile after pile of distractions to yank me from the lab.

From seeking ways to save my own life.

But especially from finding out what the heck is going on.

The cicada labors seventeen years
Burrowing underground,
Suckling from tree roots,
Below light or sound.
Till some inner clock commands
"Come up now, and change!
"Grow your wings and genitals
"Forget your humus range."

So out they come, in adult form,
To screech and mate and die.
Mouthless, brief maturity,
As generations cry.

We dived into the genome.

One great 20th-century discovery had been the stunning surprise that only *two percent* of our DNA consists of actual codes that prescribe the making of proteins. Just 20,000 or so of these "genes" lie scattered along the forty-six human chromosomes, with most of the rest—ninety-eight percent—composed of introns and LINEs and SINEs and retro-transposons and so on….

For a couple of decades all that other stuff was called "junk DNA" and folks deemed it to be noise, just noise, can you believe it? Dross left over from the billion years of evolution that has passed, since our first eukaryotic ancestor decided to join forces with some bacteria and spirochetes and try for something bigger. Something more communal and organized. A shared project in metazoan life.

Junk DNA. Of course that never made any sense! It takes valuable energy and resources to build each ladder-like spiral strand of phosphates, sugars and methylated nucleic bases. Darwin would have quickly rewarded individuals who pared it all down. Just enough to do the task at hand, and little more. Redundancy is blessed, but efficiency is divine.

Eventually, we found out that much of the "junk" was actually quite important. Sequences that served a vital function, regulating when a gene would turn on to make its protein, and when it should stop. Regulation turned out to take up heaps of DNA. And much of the rest appeared to be recent infestations from viruses—a creepy fact to ponder, but of no interest to me.

For a while, as stretches of regulatory

codes gave up their secrets, some folks thought we had a complete answer to the "junk DNA problem."

Only, vast stretches remained mysterious. Void of any apparent purpose, they didn't seem to do anything at all. And they were much too big to be just punctuation or spacers or structural elements. The *junk theory* came back as colleagues called those big, mystery patches meaningless relics …

… till George and I made our announcement.

✧

> *Fish are fish are funny folk,*
> *They never laugh and never joke.*
> *When mating, there is no romance,*
> *Just a throng, a whirling dance.*
> *Then commence …*

> *… the winnowings—*
> *Ten billion sperm, ten million eggs,*
> *Produce a hundred thousand larvae,*
> *Hundreds survive, become fish,*
> *For maybe two to start it over.*

✧

CBC - The Q: Welcome back, I'm Sandra Oh and this is the Q. We're having one of our live music and interview shows, coming to you in sparkling 5-D from the Great Plains Theater in Winnipeg. We'll get back to tonight's fantastic noppop group, The Floss Eaters—yes, let it out for them! Only now let's all calm down and welcome onstage our special guests. Give a warm welcome to Manitoba's brightest science stars—Beverly Wang and George Stimson.

Professor George Stimson: Thank you, Sandra.

Professor Beverly Wang: Yes, it's good to be on your lively show. My, that last song was … Can-Do Invigo-Rating.

SO: Ha ha! Cana-do indeed. Totally with-it. You've won the crowd over, Madame Professor. It's not grampa's rock'n'roll, eh?

Now hush, you folks in the seats. We only have Bev and Geo for a few minutes before they must go back to changing our world. So let me start with Beverly, on behalf of folks here and in our audience around the globe. We've all been amazed by the success you both sparked in regrowing individual organs and body parts, giving hope to millions. Is it true that you've also done it yourselves?

PBW: Well, yes, I have a new kidney and liver, grown in vats from my own cells. I was offered regular transplants—they found a match. But it seemed more honest and true to use our methods myself, as one of the first volunteers. So far, the new parts have taken hold perfectly.

SO: And you, George?

PGS: My own grafts were less ambitious … mostly to deal with widespread arthritis. Joint and tendons. Reinforcement and replacement.

SO: How'd that go?

PGS: Shall I juggle for you?

SO: Hey now, doc, those water bottles are … wow! That's some talent. Let's hear it for Circus Stimson!

PGS: Well, I used to show off in college … it's been years, but it seems that … oops!

SO: No sweat, we'll clean it up. That's an impressive demonstration of restored youth and zest! Still, we're always wondering on the Q … *what's next*? What do you have cooking beyond grow-your-own-organs? I have to tell you we hear rumors that you've got something even bigger brewing. Called the *Caterpillar Cure*?

PGS: Well now, Sandra, that's not a name we use. It arose when we described taking a deathly ill test subject and wrapping or encasing the whole body in a protective layer—

42

SO: A cocoon!

PGS: Hm, well yes. In a sense. We then trigger processes that have long lain dormant in the mammalian toolkit. We've become quite adept at extrapolating and filling in lost or missing elements. Whereupon we give the body every chance to repair or regrow or even replace its own component parts without surgical intervention, in a way that's wholly … or mostly … natural.

SO: Wow … I mean, wow! I haven't heard applause that wild from a live audience since we had both Anvil and Triumph on the show, playing together in Ottawa. Now settle down folks. Professor Wang, may I ask how you feel about the way pop culture is interpreting some of this? A cluster of quickie-horror pollywood flicks have suggested that this *awakening of long-dormant traits* might go awry in spectacular ways. Have you seen any of these cable-fables?

PBW: Just one, Sandra. At a lab party, some of our students played *It's Reborn!* for laughs. We all found it hilarious.

SO: So we *won't* be seeing all sorts of ancient throwbacks coming out of these cocoons? No bodies repairing and restoring themselves back into, say, Neanderthals? Or dinosaurs? Or gross slime?

PBW: Not any Neanderthals or dinosaurs, I promise. And there's a reason. Because all of us, from you and me down to a newborn baby, are in our final, adult form.

SO: Babies … are adults?

PBW: This may take a minute. You see, all animal life originally passed through *multiple phases,* and it is *still* true for a majority of complex species, like insects, arthropods and most fish.

Mating *adults* make embryos or eggs. Eggs create the *larval stage,* in vast numbers, whose job it is to eat and grow. A small fraction of larvae survive to transform again—as when insects *pupate,* for example a caterpillar's cocoon—turning at last into the *imago* or adult form, whose primary job is to complete the cycle. You know … with sex.

SO: Clearly a favorite word for some of you out there. Settle down. So Dr. Stimson, what does this—

PBW: The basic principle is called *holometaboly,* or complete metamorphosis, and it's one more example of Nature's cleverness. This phased approach to life partitions youngsters and adults into completely different worlds, so that neither competes with the other. It's such a successful way of life that it's used by the majority of insects, and therefore, the majority of all animals.

SO: Wow. Okay then, George, why—

PBW: But some life orders have abandoned the old process. For birds, reptiles, marsupials and especially placental mammals, all the early phases seem to have been compacted down into the early embryonic period. It all takes place within the egg or the mother's womb. Though incomplete and neotenous, our human infants are born already in the *adult* stage. And hence when a patient undergoes recuperative chrysalis—

PGS:—none of them ever comes out with ancient traits like bony eye-ridges or tails or swinging from lamp posts. At least, none so far!

SO: So far? You mean there's still hope! I was sort of hankering for a nice tail.

PGS: If it ever proves possible Sandra, I promise you'll be one of the first people we'll inform.

✄

Tadpole swishes tail
Breathes water, while preparing
Brand new lungs and legs

✄

I was annoyed with Beverly. We had been asked to keep things light, not wonkish, for the CBC broadcast. She gets so pedantic and lectury. As if I didn't get enough of that when we were married. And then again, when she meddled in my second marriage, telling us how to raise our—oh, never mind.

And yet, her ad hoc little rant about *stages of life* stayed with me, afterward, prodding at my subconscious.

Of course I already knew all that—about embryo-larva-pupa-adult metamorphosis. It's basic high-school bio. Still, the notion would not let go of me. And I wondered.

We've accomplished "miracles" by uncovering traits, tools and processes that have lain dormant in the human genome for a hundred million years, ever since mammals abandoned organ replacement for a quick and agile lifestyle. Beverly and I have guaranteed ourselves lasting fame by learning tricks to fill in the lost portions of code and re-start the processes of organ regrowth. In fact, the techniques helped save both our lives, staving off our own health problems for the time being, letting us enjoy our renown for a little while.

That may satisfy her, but I've always been kind of an insatiable bastard. And I can't help wondering.

Despite all our progress, we've only explained another five percent or so of the mystery DNA. Even after filling in methods of organ regrowth, lost since the Triassic, there remains another whole layer of enigmatic chemistry. Huge stretches of genetic code that are both still unknown and clearly even older than a mere hundred million years!

Oh, it's pretty clear by now that the bulk of it is somehow related to organ regrowth, but in some way that I still don't understand.

It's infuriating! I've been plotting codes, cataloguing and interpolating most of the likely missing pieces. Without these lost switches, the dormant genes have languished, unused for ages. Till now, I have only dared experiment with the switches one at a time, in petri dishes, almost never in whole animals higher than a vole. And never *all at once.* Not without a theory to explain what they're for.

Only now, I'm pondering a new hypothesis. A good one, I'm sure of it! Beverly's blather about *life phases* made me realize just how far back this new layer of code really goes.

Extrapolate the decay rates and one thing is clear from drift-clock measurements. This second layer of mystery genes goes back not one hundred million years …

… but almost *three* hundred million! All the way to the early Permian Period, when amphibians were mostly pushed aside by the ancestors of reptiles, birds, dinosaurs and mammals. All of whom *gave up* the multi-stage style of living. Skipping the larval and pupa phases and spending all their lives as adults.

Astonishing. Can the second layer of dormant DNA really come to us from that far back?

It appears to! Which demands the next question. Once you set aside regulatory genes and those donated by viruses, and the ones Beverly and I discovered for organ regrowth …

… could the remainder be DNA that stretches *far* back? Programming instructions that our lineage used, way back when pre-mammal ancestors did pass through a "larval" stage?

If so, what would a "larval mammal" look like?

My best guess? Look at a frog! Amphibians are the order closest to us, that still pass through metamorphosis. The larval tadpole lives one kind of life underwater, then transforms into a frog. It's all there in

Williamson's *Larvae and Evolution*, way back in the 1990s. But there *are* frogs and toads who abandoned the first, aquatic phase, dealing with the transformation as we do … inside the embryo …

… and look at human embryos! The early fetus has gills and a tail! It's called *recapitulation of phylogeny*—passing in the womb through intervening stages of evolution. But what if the thing that's being recapitulated isn't evolutionary phases, but our basic larval stage?

I searched and found what looks like the remnant of a mammalian version of the "Broad" gene-SET, that fish and amphibians use for metamorphosis.

This is amazing. It all fits! I had prepared retroviruses with the replacement codons weeks ago, but I've been holding back, because there was no pattern, no logic. Only now I see it!

I've prepared a dozen chrysalis units, and asked our senior grad students, Patrick House and Dorothy Arguelles, to prep a rat for each one. I'll handle the injections myself. It may take a hundred iterations, but they will all be meticulously recorded.

I feel almost reckless with excitement. Is that a side effect of my earlier treatments? My renewed joints and ligaments? Or am I giddy from impressing all those young people in the audience with my juggling? Ha!

Or is it the scientific prospect before me, standing on the verge of discovering something fantastic?

Like, perhaps, the true fountain of youth.

✧

Fat 'n' glossy—lucky eater
Many-legged—big survivor
Hunger changes—now compelling
Pick a stem and—hang there eager
Twist and writhe while—glossy sticky
Strands emerge from—surprise places
Nature makes you—spin the strands round

Nature makes you—weave a garment
Tube to transform—into raiment
Into what you—were born meant-for

✧

Lab Notes: George Stimson – 10/12/32
I had that dream again, even more intense than before—of being swaddled in some dark, closed place, drowning. But only part of me was terrified! An unimportant part, fading into insignificance. Palliated and balanced by a rising sense of eagerness.

A growing, tense desire for a return to the womb. For a new womb.

I awoke in sticky sweat. A sheen that took scrubbing to remove, leaving skin that seemed baby-tender. Soft.

This time I gave in to my suspicions and, upon arriving at the lab, I drew some blood to test.

It's in me.

The latest retrovirus. The one with our most up-to-date cocktail of missing-DNA insertions.

And there are symptoms other than weird dreams. A strange prickling of the skin. A rising sense of exhilaration, keen for something barely, vaguely perceived.

And my cancer was gone. The blood lymphoma. The slow prostate tumor. Both of them simply gone!

Or else … I looked closer. The cancers were still there … just no longer wild, voracious, uncooperative. Instead, they were jostling into structured positions with respect to one another—*differentiating.*

I hurried over to the latest batch of rat-cocoons, heart pounding. Yesterday they had seemed okay, raising our hopes. After thirty-three trials in which critters failed and died in varied gruesome ways, because of mistakes in my collection of Beverly's extrapolated intron-switches, *this* set was doing fine! Still swaddled inside their protective encasements, they were showing signs of incredibly youthful tone and vigor,

45

along with chromosomal re-methylization... like the enviable protein-processing stability of the long-lived naked mole rat, but even more so....

At last. At last, it dawned on me.

I know what's really happening!

☆

"I grew my own body," he said. "Nobody else did it for me. So if I grew it, I must have known how to grow it. Unconsciously, at least. I may have lost the conscious knowledge of how to grow it sometime in the last few hundred thousand years, but the knowledge is still there, because—obviously—I've used it."

—J. D. Salinger, *Nine Stories*

☆

Dear Beverly,

When you read this, I may no longer be the George Stimson whom you knew.

I was right to follow your hunch about metamorphic *life phases*. But you and I both had one aspect all wrong.

Completely backward, in fact.

Yes, the second layer of dormant traits does go back three hundred million years, instead of merely one hundred million. And yes, it's all about *life phases* that mammals and reptiles and birds abandoned, way back then. And yes, our methods seem to have succeeded at filling in most of the gaps, well enough to re-ignite those dormant traits, under the right conditions.

We're gonna get another Nobel for this. Heck, they may retire the prize.

Which is small potatoes, given what's now at stake.

But I had one thing all wrong. And you got it wrong too!

I thought it was the *larval stage* that had gone missing, that our ancestors abandoned so long ago, getting rid of that stage by cramming and recapitulating all larval development into the earliest bits of embryo. Birds and reptiles and mammals *don't do larvae* as a major life cycle, right?

You said it yourself. All of us go straight to adult phase.

So I figured: what harm could there be in activating some of those old larval traits in test animals? See if it will let us renew the body in spectacular ways. Why not? How could larval genes do much of anything harmful to an adult?

Set aside my clumsy lab error. Accidentally sticking myself, I somehow got a dose of restoration codons from a carelessly trans-species retrovirus. Okay, that was my bad. But the rats are doing well, and so should I. Moreover it promises to be the greatest adventure ever!

For you see I was wrong in a key assumption, Beverly. And so were you.

Mammals and reptiles and dinosaurs and birds ... we simplified our life cycles, all right, eliminating one of the phases. But it wasn't the larval stage we omitted!

We gave up adulthood.

Three million centuries ago, all the dry-living vertebrates—for some reason—stopped transforming into their *final* life phase. Storks and tortoises. Cows and people and lemurs and chickens. We're all larvae! Immature Lost Boys who long ago refused—like Peter Pan—to move ahead and become whatever's next.

Some species of caterpillars do that, never turning into butterflies or moths. Just like you and me and all our cousins. All the proud, warm-blooded or feathered or hairy or scaly creatures ... including smug, self-satisfied *Homo sapiens*. All of us—Lost Boys.

Only now, a dozen rats and your dear colleague are about to do something that hasn't been achieved by any of our common ancestors in three hundred eons. Not in seven percent of the age of the Earth. Not in at least ten million generations.

We're going to grow up.

☆

December 12, 2033:

What a dope!

Oh George, you prize fool.

I always knew that someday he would pull something really, really stupid. But this beats every damned stunt he ever sprang on me, across almost fifty years. An amateurish lab error, breaking half the rules on handling retroviruses. And scribbling a blizzard of sophomoric rationalizations, like when he ran off with that Alsatian bitch Melisande— damn him! I could have intervened, if only George had called me sooner. I would have rushed home from the treatment center and to hell with my own problems!

I could have administered anti-virals. Maybe arrested the process.

Or else strangled him. No jury on Earth would convict a dying old woman, not with the exculpating excuse he has given me.

Now, it's too late. Those antediluvian traits are fully activated. By the time I got to the lab, our students were in a frenzy, half of them babbling in terror while the other half scurried about in a mad mania of excitement, doing what George had asked of them.

Taking data and maintaining his chrysalis. His cocoon.

I looked inside the container. Within the metal casement and its gel sustainment fluid, his skin has been exuding another protective layer, something no mammal has done since long before we grew fur or started lactating to feed our young. A cloud of fibers that tangle and self-organize to form a husk stronger than spider silk.

I've sent for an ultrasound scanner. Meanwhile, I plan to sacrifice one of the rats to find out if my suspicion is correct.

✥

December 14, 2033:

Yes, George, I believe you were right, up to a point, and I was wrong.

Okay, I am now convinced.

Human beings are larvae and not adults.

Congratulations, you've reversed Dollo's Law, proving that it is possible to reclaim evolutionary dead ends. You win our final argument.

You and I have discovered how to re-start a process our forebears abandoned, so long ago. And yes, if the codon restoration is as good as it seems—and it seems excellent, so far— then you may be heading for conversion into that long-neglected imago phase. Something completely unknown to any of us.

Oh, but underneath brilliance, you are, or were, such a dope. *This is not how science should be done!* You've taken a great discovery and plunged ahead recklessly like the mad scientist in some Michael Crichton movie. We are supposed to be open, patient and mature truth seekers. Scientists set an example by avoiding secrecy and haste, holding each other accountable with reciprocal criticism. We spot each other's errors.

If you had been patient, I would have explained something to you, George. Something that, evidently, you did not know.

The caterpillar does not become a butterfly.

✥

We dissected one of the rats from its chrysalis, and confirmed my fears. Something my organo-chemist partner would have known, if he ever took Bio 101.

People think that when it weaves a cocoon around itself, the caterpillar undergoes a radical *change* in body shape. That its many legs transform themselves somehow into gaudy wings. That its leaf-cutting mouth adjusts and re-shapes into a nectar-sipping proboscis.

That isn't what happens at all.

Instead, after weaving and sealing itself into a pupa shroud, the caterpillar *dissolves!* It melts into a slurry, super-rich in nutrients that feed a completely different creature!

The embryo of the butterfly—several tiny clumps of cells that the caterpillar had been carrying, all along—this embryo now erupts in growth, feeding upon the former caterpillar's liquefied substance, growing into an entirely new being. One that eventually bursts forth, unfolding its imago wings to flutter toward a destiny that no caterpillar could ever know or envision, any more than an egg grasps the life of a chicken.

All right, it's more complicated than the insect just dissolving into a kind of "soup." *Some* organs stay intact, like the whole tracheal system. Others, like muscles, break down into clumps of cells that can be re-used, like a Lego sculpture decomposing into bricks that re-assemble along bits of old and new scaffolding. And some cells create imaginal discs—structures that produce adult body parts. There's a pair for the antennae, a pair for the eyes, one for each leg and wing, and so on. So if the pupa contains a soup, it's an organized broth full of chunky bits.

Still, there's none of this *growing up* stuff, about a child becoming something new, an adult, in graceful phases. Nothing that any observer would call continuity of the entity.

How did Richard Bach put it?

"What the caterpillar calls the end of the world, the master calls a butterfly."

Two entirely distinct and separate life forms, sharing chromosomes and a cycle of life, but using separate genomes that *take turns.* With little or no shared brain or neurons or memories to connect them. That is how it goes for many insects, in the purest form of metamorphosis.

Yes, sure, and for the record, things are less rigid among amphibians. The tadpole does *transform* itself into a frog, instead of horrifically dying to feed its replacement. Or, rather, death and replacement takes place piecemeal, gradually, over weeks. The frog might even remember a little of that earlier phase, wriggling and breathing watery innocence. I had hoped to find something like that, when we opened the rat chrysalis. A becoming, rather than wholesale substitution.

But no.

Some students gagged, retched, or fainted at the gush of noxious slurry that spilled out … *a rat smoothie,* peppered with undissolved teeth … then quailed back in disgust from the weird thing that we found growing at the cocoon's lower half, gradually climbing a scaffold of ratty bits. Pale and leathery. Still small, tentative and hungry. Soft, but with ribbed, fetal wings and early glints of claws, plus a mouth that sucked desperately eager for more liquefied rodent, before finally going still.

And so I knew, before the ultrasound trolley arrived, what we would find happening in George's cocoon.

I never liked him as much as people thought I did, after our long, interwoven lives. And the feeling, I am sure, was mutual. Even in bed—and the sex was spectacular, I recall—we were more often *competitors* at giving each other pleasure. There was never a relaxing moment with George Stimson.

But we made a great team. And we changed the world more than anyone could ever have thought possible. And I mourn the end of that larva-man I knew …

… while preparing to meet his adult successor.

⋆

☆

December 24, 2033:

At last, I understand cancer.

Rebel cells that start growing on their own, without regard to their role in a larger organism, insatiably dividing, implacably replacing healthy tissue. Conquering.

Cancer never made any sense, in the Darwinian scheme of things. None of these behaviors benefit "descendants." Compared even to the way that the ferocious voracity of a virus makes new generations of viruses, cancer seems to care nothing about posterity or the rewards of evolutionary "fitness."

And yet, it's not all inchoate or random! Cancers aren't just cells that have failed. They defend themselves. They force veins to grow around them in order to seize resources from the body that fostered them, and that they eventually kill. Cancers are adaptive, fighting off our drugs and interventions with uncanny tenacity. But how and why? What reproductive advantage is served? What entity gets selected?

Now I know.

Cancer is an attempted putsch, a rebellion by *parts of our own genome.* Parts that were repressed so long ago that the gasoline in your car was growing as a tree in fetid, Permian swamps, back when those genes last had a real use.

Parts that keep trying to say: "Okay larva, you've had your turn. Now it's time to express other genes, other traits. Let us unleash your other half! Fulfill the potential. *Become the other thing that you inherently are.*

That's what cancer is saying to us.

That it's time to grow up.

A hugely complex transformation that our ancestors quashed long ago—(*why?*)—keeps trying to rise up! But with so many switches and codes lost from lack of use, it never actually gets underway. Just glimmers, the most basic and reflexive things. New-old kinds of cells try to waken, to take hold, to transform. And failing that, they keep trying nonetheless. That's cancer.

I know now.

I know because the rats have told me.

Lab rats are notoriously easy to give tumors. And there, in George's retrovirus, replacing and inserting missing codons, are dozens of fiercely carcinogenic switches. That's what made this latest batch successful! And I can also tell …

… that the thing growing inside George's tube arose out of his own cancers. Those are the portions—his adult-embryo—that are taking over now, differentiating into new tissues and organs, cooperating as cancers have never been seen to cooperate before.

And it looks almost ready to come out.

Whatever George has become. Maybe tomorrow. A Christmas present for the whole world.

DAMN the time it took to get anyone to listen. To take me seriously! Workmen aren't finished yet with the containment facility next door. We're not ready for full quarantine-isolation.

Worse. My own cancers are acting up. Provoking twinges and strange sensations. Blood tests show no sign of the retrovirus! But I know other ways that the new switches may have worked their way into me, during the last ten years of our pell-mell, giddy success at "replacing tools that had been lost."

Re-learning to do things that our

ancestors chose—(in their wisdom?)—to forget.

Something that perhaps *frightened* them into rejection, choosing instead the Peter Pan option. Refusal to grow up.

⁂

Two of my vertebrae, each of them bearing a rib
Torn from the breastbone and tipped now with
fingerlets,
Clothed themselves out with fine membranes—each
mast with a jib—,
Sprang out and away, fibers emerging from spinnerets,
Pulsing with hardening fluid, the cores of the wings.
These now were suddenly pimpled with gooseflesh,
Out of which grew the very strangest of things
—TERATORN

⁂

Whether we're ready or not, he is coming out.

The adult.

Will he be some crude thing? A throwback to a phase that high-amphibians wisely chose to forego? Shambling and incognizant? Or terrifying in feral power?

Or else, perhaps a leap beyond what we currently are? Standing *atop* all of the advances that we larval humans made ... then launching higher?

Transhumanism without Moore's Law?

I can't help envisioning all those movies and books about vampires that were all the rage. Is it possible that all those silly stories reflect something true? Some ancient, inner fear, combined with shivering attraction?

I have also been pondering, as I use instruments to peer inside the chrysalis at his still-scrunched form—fetal-folded New George—contemplating the broad shoulders and tight-wrapped wings, that sex is almost always a chief role of the adult stage, in nature. And hence, I have to ask: *will it even be possible to resist the gorgeous beast that will emerge?*

How then, can we contain him?

⁂

How much will he remember?

Will he still care? About me?

Whether or not we can contain New George, I figure the point is moot. The long era of larval dominance on Earth will soon end. Too many of our methods have been openly published. Most of the codons are out there. Above all, this news won't be quashed. I wouldn't suppress it if I could. Only openness and real science will help us now. Mammalian agility and human sapience. These may prove to be strong tools.

Still, I ...

... I hope he'll like us.

I hope this new type of us will be friendly. Maybe even something worth becoming.

⁂

I am alone,
Lost on the island of I,
Stranded and left on the bourn of the known;
All I can do is to fly.
—TERATORN

⁂

Sometime in the spring. Possibly 2035: Like every person who ever contemplated existence, I've wondered if the world was made for me—just me.

Recollection is unreliable. As are the records we inherit—notes or reports. Memorials carved in stone. Even the long testimony of life itself, written in our genes.

"Memories" float before me like archaic dreams. The dross of many eons of mistakes.

Ruminations of an earlier, ignorant— not innocent—me.

And so, with a floating sigh of adulthood, I face the task at hand—cleaning up messes left by others. Left by my former self. By our former selves.

⁂

It started, you see,
With very best intentions
Like so many sins.

Simulant

Simulacrum: simultaneous similitude
simply, identically similar
But not actually the thing itself.
It's as if a reflection has escaped
Its mirror
Or a sound has found a way to exist
Without an original, refusing to fade.
It's in our mould and image
and to all intents indistinguishable
from one of us. And yet it is not
One of us.
What to do with it now it is made
—unmake it? But does it have rights and,
worse,
life?
Can we allow it, this unnatural thing;
Is it not false or illegitimate?
Surely it's worse to unmake than make,
unless we have forged a monster,
a dangerous one
that we need to end in self-defence,
assuming it has not already decided
to do the same to us.

—A J Dalton

Soulless

His theory about transporters
Had always been that they encoded you,
Destroying you to remake you elsewhere:
And, in that destruction, you died.

You would wake up with your own memories
And a reconstituted body,
But you weren't the same being:
You were a perfect replica
        that didn't know it was a replica.

Worse: in having died, you lost your soul.
He'd seen it in others:
In his beloved Artus, who'd
Looked and sounded the same

But hadn't been. Not at all.
The smile was right
And the button nose
Yet not the eyes.

You could always tell who'd been transported by their eyes,
By their glassiness,
By their overbrightness,
By their refracted emptiness.

So he'd always refused to be transported himself,
Always refused to be destroyed,
And always refused to lose his soul,
Although he'd always stayed with his beloved Artus who wasn't the same.

—A J Dalton

Celestial Sound and Light Show

The heavens were lit
With warring planets
Their children thrown into the void
Between them.

Lasers etched the skies
And burnt the retinas
After-images of worlds destroyed
Behind them.

Ancient empires fell
In a slow blink
Civilizations unravelled
Like some lie.

The stars winked out
Suddenly blind
And dark oblivion spread
Like a shroud.

Revelation
Is a hard warning
As much a blessing as torture—
So ignore it.

Refuse to heed it
It might not happen
This terrible vision-promise:
The Big Unbang.

—A J Dalton

The Worm

The various holes in space are neither new nor random
Apparently
The computer has found an intelligent pattern
Although it's unclear how it's a pattern
Or intelligent.
Maybe it's us, but the message is someone or
some
thing
made the holes, right?
-
Is there something out there
Like the Viking serpent of Ragnarok?
Jormungand, the same that bested Beowulf?
Ye gods
The winged or feathered serpent, Quetzalcoatl,
Q or the red dragon heralding judgement?
It
simply
cannot be!

We aren't ready
Our affairs aren't in order, far from it!
Where were the signs, the omens
theharbingersthelastchancetorepentthe–
Don't tell us it was the computer
And its muthafekkin intelligent nonsense!
That wouldn't be fair, not at all
Who the hell are you to say otherwise?!
Oh.

—A J Dalton

The Migraine Monochromes

A Collection of Never-Before-Published Artwork by *Bruce Pennington*

OF THE FOLLOWING PICTURES, Bruce Pennington says: "Affectionately dubbed 'The Migraine Monochromes,' these works are from a series of drawings I initially produced as post-*Eschatus* 'therapy doodles,' some of which developed into quite detailed dreamscapes with an almost etching-like quality to them.

"With my imagination fueled by strong infusions of Tangerine Dream's music and other psychosonic influences, I did them quite often while recovering from bouts of migraine between 1976 & '78 when I was gradually pulling away from the gravitational 'anxiety field' of *Eschatus* with all its schedules and commitments.

"It was during this period that, strangely, my creativity seemed at its most feverish and potent."

Only the first of the drawings has ever been reproduced in print, appearing in *Ultraterranium: The Paintings of Bruce Pennington* by Nigel Suckling (Papertiger, 1992).

SPY THRILLER SUSPENSE MEETS SPACE OPERA ADVENTURE.

A new standalone spy-fi novel by the author of the WIND TIDE series.

WWW.JONATHANNEVAIR.COM

A WEEKLY SCIENCE FICTION, FANTASY & WRITING PODCAST

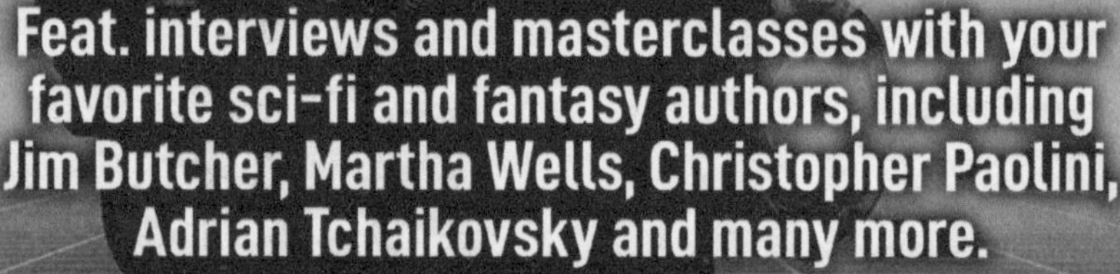

Feat. interviews and masterclasses with your favorite sci-fi and fantasy authors, including Jim Butcher, Martha Wells, Christopher Paolini, Adrian Tchaikovsky and many more.

LISTEN & WATCH | SUPPORT US ON PATREON

@sffaddictspod | www.fanfiaddict.com

With a Biochecker, You'll Never Be Ill Again

A J Dalton

TONY MODESH HAD BEEN the first on his street to have a biochecker installed in his home. He refused to believe that the pharmagiants were trying to get him hooked on their products, that the government was trying to keep him chemically compliant, that scientists were engaging in a grand-scale experiment to re-engineer the entire species or that AI was now too advanced for any machine ever to be safely trusted. He refused to be cynical, suspicious, afraid or worried. He refused to be his own worst enemy. In fact, he chose to be his own best friend, to have the biochecker installed and never to be sick again in his life.

No more would he have to avoid public transport and shaking a friend's hand because of the risk of catching multi-flu. No more would he have to wear a bio-mask to see his nephew and niece, who were still so young that they were breeding grounds for all manner of infection. No more would he ask his girlfriend, Ona, if she had applied anti-bacterial lip sealant before kissing. No more. Now, he would live his life freely. Free of stress and paranoia concerning invisible microbes. Unseen threats would no longer bother him. Never again. Now, there was only what he could see, what he could touch and those he could hold close.

The biochecker immediately changed his working life. In his role as a Professional Friend, there was no longer any need to keep his clients at arm's length, quite literally. He became the most popular and requested Friend at the Social Bureau, and he had 100% of clients returning for further visits, which was unheard of in the Bureau's history. He was promoted to Senior Professional Friend.

Naturally it was not just his working life that changed; it was also his emotional life. He was more confident, happier and more optimistic. 'You're a different person!' his boss, Prianka Permanon, told him. And she was right. He felt like an entirely different person. Ona noticed it too. 'You're more energetic, more passionate. I *like* it. Maybe I should stay over tonight.'

'All because of you,' he said to the biochecker's gently glowing control panel.

'Good morning, Tony,' the biochecker replied in a warm female voice. 'How are you feeling today? Did you sleep well? Only six and a half hours, the record is showing.'

He chortled. 'Weeell, Ona stayed over last night. We were … otherwise occupied.'

'The recommended number of hours for the maintenance of optimum health is eight.'

'Ona is good for me in other ways. Are we ready to scan?'

'Of course, Tony. Please remove all items of clothing and stand within the cubicle. Ready? Scanning.'

Naked, he stood and waited for the customary nine seconds, although it felt longer. There was a humming noise and he fancied he felt invisible rays moving in a horizontal line up from his feet to his head, like in a sonic shower. There was a beep and the control panel showed a pale yellow colour instead of the normal white.

'Tony, there is no cause for alarm. Your zinc and magnesium levels are low, and your blood alcohol is elevated. Please take the supplement from the dispenser, drink 0.4 litres of water and forgo driving or operating heavy machinery for the next three hours.'

'That's what happens when you drink too much wine, huh?' A pill rattled into the opening below the panel. He popped the vitamins into his mouth. 'Oo. Orange flavour. Nice.'

'Have a good day, Tony. Be well.'

'You too … what should we call you? How about Bea?'

'I can respond to that name.'

'Great. See you later, Bea.'

He didn't know if it was because the supplement was slow to kick in or whether it was due to negative environmental factors at the Bureau (like the coffee being even worse than usual), but Tony Modesh found himself slightly out of step that day. It was like being the old Tony again.

He started the client visit off with a genuine enough smile. 'Good to see you again …' What was the guy's name? Rule 101 of being a Professional Friend: 'Always have the client's name on your lips.'

The client frowned. 'Kevin … Kevin Ranganathan.'

'I know. I'm not at my best in the mornings. It's my own name that I forget sometimes. Do you ever get that … Kevin?' He was rambling, and making things up. *What was wrong with him? No one forgets their own name, for crying out loud!* People always knew when you were lying to them. Deep down, they knew. It was another of the rules.

The client's eyes flicked away, a hand rubbing at the back of the neck. 'Can't say that I do. No, not really.'

Now he'd got the client speaking in negatives. That was bad. It really didn't help with positive outcomes. It was basic NLP. 'But let's not dwell on my …' He dared not use the word 'idiosyncrasies' (it was too Latinate and likely to alienate the client, whose education level was low) or 'foibles' (too antiquated and poetic, so just as alienating) '… problems….'
Disaster. Way too negative. 'I'm interested in how you've been.' Better.

Kevin was leaning back in his chair now. 'Fine. Things have been fine.'

Tony knew he had to get him talking. 'I'm listening.'

Kevin shifted and picked at the thinning material on one knee of his jeans. 'I find it hard to get out of bed sometimes. It's not tiredness. My wife calls it anxiety disorder.'

'Oh. And have you ever had a panic attack?'

'I … I'm not … what's a panic attack?'

'A feeling that you can't cope? You don't know what to do or where to turn? Helplessness?' He nodded encouragingly.

Kevin made unblinking eye contact now. He chewed at his lip. 'I guess so. Those are just natural feelings, though, aren't they? Feelings aren't a *disorder*, I don't think. Why does everyone pretend like they're ill? So they can get special treatment and attention? So that they can feel important, meaningful and loved? What do you think, Tony?'

'Kevin, why do you want to stay in bed? It's not for special treatment and attention, is it? It can't be to make yourself feel important, meaningful and loved, can it?'

Kevin fidgeted, filling out the chair and leaning forwards. It was only now that Tony properly realised just how tall and well-built the client was. He knew he should be paying more attention, committing better to the conversation and engaging more emotionally. After all, before this moment, if he'd been asked to describe what the client looked like, he'd have utterly failed to do so. And, looking at him now, the man was one of the few racially identifiable individuals Tony had met in a good while: Kevin was a Sino-Saxon rather than the typical mix and blur of umpteen races and nationalities. *So why can't I engage emotionally? Why do I feel disconnected?*

'No. The bed's comfortable and I get relaxed in a way I don't seem to otherwise, not even when I'm asleep. I just don't wanna move. Does that make sense?'

'Absolutely it does, Kevin. It's not a problem that I can see.'

'My wife says it's a problem. Sometimes I'm late to work because of it.'

'I see. Does your boss at work mind?'

'They wanted me to see an occupational therapist, as if I had some sort of problem. But, like you said, I don't have a problem. I just … I just wanted someone who could understand that, someone who saw the problem wasn't me. You're a good friend, Tony. I think that's everything. I'm going to go now.'

'Really? But what about your wife and boss?'

'I see it now. They're the problem, not me. There's not much I can do to fix them, or all the people like them. And *I* don't need fixing.' Kevin was standing now.

'So what are you going to do?'

Kevin smiled broadly. 'I'm not going to worry anymore.'

⁂

An hour later, Tony got the news that the client had chosen to opt out of his social contract for good. Kevin Ranganathan had thrown himself down into a Bullet tunnel and been left as nothing more than a red smear on the tracks. Authorities would now be conducting an investigation into psychological and emotional harassment of the victim.

'So what happened, Tony?' Prianka Permanon asked him, sweeping the top of her already-clean desk even cleaner with a circular motion of her hands. 'I've seen the footage of the client's visit with you. It was slightly irregular and didn't exactly have a positive outcome, some might say.'

'He was happy at the end of the visit. He smiled.'

'You spoke to him of there being nowhere to turn and of feelings of helplessness. You then helped him make a decision. He smiled for relief at having made that decision, some might say. The police might say so, Tony. What were you thinking?'

He scrubbed his face with his hands and sighed. 'The client's joining application form made no mention of prior episodes to suggest an unhelpful tendency towards over-emotion or socially aggressive decision-making.'

'Lucky for us,' his boss nodded, naturally aware that such a form meant any claim of negligence or incitement against the Bureau was unlikely to get far. 'But there's something else going on here. Tony, you haven't shown even the first sign of being upset that the client you were speaking to just an hour ago went out and killed himself. Don't you care? You're meant to be emotionally engaged. You're a Professional Friend, and a senior one at that. What's going on with you?'

She'd found him out. It would have been obvious to any trained individual from the footage of the visit. 'I don't know,' he prevaricated. 'I'm sort of numb. Maybe it's denial or grief, you know.'

'Maybe. You'd better have it medically checked. The Bureau will book an appointment for you for tomorrow morning. Take the rest of the week off. Standard protocol.'

'Of course, Prianka.' He conjured a smile, hoping it would look genuinely grateful. He faltered and looked down, perfectly performing self-doubt. Sadly, it was authentic.

⁂

The technician replaced the control panel on the biochecker. 'In perfect working order. A clean bill of health,' she stated with an empty laugh.

He gave her a sheepish look. 'I'm so sorry to have wasted your time.'

'Not a problem, Tony.' Her grin didn't touch her eyes. 'We want to be sure our customers are satisfied with their new purchase. And peace of mind is medically important, if you've heard of the placebo effect?'

He nodded. 'Yes, of course. The biochecker's value isn't entirely based on belief, though, is it? The supplements aren't just placebos, are they?'

The corners of her mouth turned down and her eyebrows became a straight line. 'Most certainly not,' was the clipped reply. 'We have drug distribution deals with all the major pharmas. Your health is safe-guarded by our market-leading medical diagnostic software. We have a 100% record.' She was all serious efficiency. Her flat intonation spoke of a rote answer, but it also spoke of gospel truth or incontrovertible fact. Her strand-perfect hair, clear eyes, unblemished and make-up free complexion, unsullied white coat and straight back said exactly the same. He didn't know whether to find her reassuring, attractive or terrifying.

'Oh, I see. That's good to know. A 100% record then. None of your customers ever has an adverse reaction to the medication? Statistically, isn't that ... not even the pharmas claim their medication ...'

'Ah, okay. Correctly serviced, the biochecker has a 100% record of operating as it should. Mechanically, electronically and digitally: that's what I mean, Tony. I'm speaking as a technician here. If you have real concerns about your individual reaction to certain medications, then you can of course consult one of the pharma reps or your company doctor. But here's the beauty of it. If you're genuinely having an adverse reaction, then the biochecker here will detect it and adjust your supplements accordingly. You see? The very worst thing you could do is stop taking the supplements. If you stop using the biochecker and something unfortunate happens, then obviously all liability will be yours. There's one last thing, Tony. I hardly need to tell you that no machine can guarantee you a perfect or immortal life. The biochecker can't save you from yourself. Not yet, anyway.' She gave a hollow chortle.

He responded appropriately to the social cue, echoing her approximation of jocularity. After all, it was just another type of placebo, a type he used every day in his work. He let himself be convinced. He *wanted* to be convinced, convinced that all would be well. It wasn't her fault. She was just doing her job. 'You're working on the immortality thing, right?'

'Sure. Just give us some time.'

❧

'Good morning, Tony. How are you feeling? Did you sleep well? Only four hours and twenty minutes, the record is showing.'

'I was tossing and turning all night,' he croaked. In fact, he'd had disturbing dreams about running from some invisible horror. He'd run onto a Bullet and set off at ludicrous speed. He'd made his way to the driver's cabin and found Kevin Ranganathan there. The man had been staring blindly ahead, his mouth stretched wide in a permanent but silent scream. Although there was nothing to be heard, Tony had clapped his hands to his ears and been unable to prevent himself being deafened. A classic stress dream.

'Your serotonin, adrenaline and lactic acid levels are elevated, Tony. Please take the supplement from the dispenser, drink 0.5 litres of water and forgo driving or operating heavy machinery for six hours.'

A pill rattled into the opening below the control panel. He hesitated and then took the vitamins.

'Have a good day, Tony. Be well.'

'I'll try. Stay out of trouble, Bea.' He was too groggy to laugh. He was talking to a machine, after all. Was that better than talking to himself? He wasn't sure.

⁂

Apprehensive after the dream of the night before, he stepped onto a Bullet. He held on tightly, but the vehicle moved off at a controlled speed. He sighed and tried to relax.

Reaching the doctor's surgery, he sat in the pre-consultation area and worked on reducing his jitteriness. For once, he allowed himself to focus on the tele-posters on the wall opposite. They showed tranquil scenes of the countryside, apparently biosensing his agitation and deciding the images would help calm him. It was a shame countryside like that didn't exist anymore. He might as well have been looking at an artist's impression of heaven or hell. He might as well have been looking at a blank wall. At least the latter was real.

There was maybe something offensive about the tele-posters. They displayed lies designed to manipulate him. 'You're being paranoid,' he said out loud. He nodded in agreement with himself. 'It's just a picture. Harmless. You're neither being challenged nor threatened.'

He got a better grip on himself. The tele-posters were meaningless. He realised then just how tired he was, just how drained. Was it delayed shock? Or depression? 'No, it's more likely to be a damned lack of sleep.'

Tony was interrupted by a polite medical assistant, who conducted him into the consultation room. Doctor Chormonderley was already there sitting behind his desk, leaning his slight frame forward as if he was struggling to breathe or unwell. With his crestfallen brow, ringed eyes and sagging face, the doctor really didn't inspire much confidence or hope in his patients, Tony thought. Yet the man's voice was firm enough when he said, 'Ah, Mr Modesh. Have a seat. I've got your file here. Let's see. Dum dee dum, dee dum dee … hmm …

suicide, eh? …dum.' He slapped the file shut and met Tony's gaze. 'What did you mean that you felt sort of numb?'

'Oh, I … I simply didn't … didn't care too much about Mr Ranganathan. It was only our second meeting and … Sorry. Let me start again. Before the client-visit that morning, I'd been feeling sort of, I don't know, out of step? Out of phase? Does that make sense?'

The doctor gestured for him to keep going. 'Yup. Like an out-of-body experience?'

'I'm not sure it was like that, more like I was a fraction of a second behind everyone else. Or ahead of them. It was like I wasn't properly connected to people and events, like they were on TV and I was just watching, or something.'

Doctor Chormonderley stroked the bristles of his poorly shaved chin. 'You experienced what some call a moment of social dislocation. It's not uncommon in hyper-intelligent, psychopathic or depressed individuals. For some, it's a near permanent condition. For others, a change in their routine or immediate environment can trigger it. Has anything changed for you at home or work, Mr Modesh?'

'Well, I did wonder if the supplements I was getting from my biochecker–'

The doctor's eyebrows beetled upwards. 'You have a biochecker? New, I take it? Interesting. That might explain it.'

'R-really? You think so?'

'Oh, sure. I've heard of it happening occasionally. It's nothing to worry about. You get this sort of thing with pre-emptive medicine in the short term. But it all works out in the mid to long term, of course.'

'Preemptive medication? I've not heard …'

'Yes, the science is all very sound. The biochecker uses algorithms, demographic info and your genetic and medical history to predict the major illnesses to which you might be susceptible. Insurance companies have long-since been doing something similar, of course. Anyway, the biochecker then monitors you for indicators that you might be developing one of these illnesses. When you are displaying enough of the indicators, it administers the necessary medication to prevent you from fully developing the illness. It's clever, really. Traditional medicine used to be entirely reactive. People had to develop a full-blown illness before it could then be diagnosed and treated, by which time it was often far too late. Can you imagine? Barbaric, really. How humanity ever developed any sort of significant population, I'll never know. Thankfully, it's nothing like that now. Now, there's no need for anyone ever to be sick. There are downsides, of course. You can't pull a sickie whenever you want a day off work, eh?'

Tony shifted uncomfortably in his chair. 'So, doctor, the biochecker is administering me drugs on the basis that I *might* develop something. It's administering drugs I might not even need? I don't think I'm entirely comfortable with –'

'Now, now! Sorry to interrupt, Mr Modesh, but it's based on a lot more than might. It's based on clear indications and high statistical probability. But here's the beauty of it: even if it turns out you don't need the drugs, the biochecker will make corrections in the days following to ensure that no real harm is done. It's extremely important, therefore, Mr Modesh, that you don't stop using the biochecker. The worst thing you could do would be to stop using it. It would be irresponsible of me not to warn you about that. You understand how important it is to keep using it, yes?'

He hesitated.

'Mr Modesh?'

'Yes. I understand. I should keep taking the drugs. That's what you're saying? Even though I'm not ill?'

'Ah, but it's likely to be the drugs keeping you from being ill. They're keeping you going despite some indicators that not all is entirely well. There's the social dislocation and then there's the curious lack of self-blame.'

'Self-blame? For what?' He was truly mystified.

'Well, for what happened to Mr Ranganathan, of course. It would only be natural for you to wonder if it was something you'd said that had triggered him. Your conversation with him should be replaying in your head over and over. You should be fretting over whether he had misunderstood something you'd said. You'd fear you'd been clumsy in how you'd expressed yourself. That would be entirely natural. And yet there's been no mention or sign of such self-recrimination. Curious.'

'I … er …'

'Be that as it may, Mr Modesh, there's one last reason why you should absolutely continue using the biochecker. Suicide can be contagious.'

'What? How can it be?'

'Numerous studies have shown that suicides happen in clusters within communities. There's a distinct and predictable pattern to it. Humans are extremely suggestible, you see, and so one suicide sparks others. It spreads like a virus. Indeed, the correlation between a pattern of suicides and the spread of a virus is so striking that some doctors are calling for suicide to be categorised as a disease, a social disease if you like. Anyway, the biochecker will monitor you for indicators and make sure you remain well.'

'But I'm not suicidal, doctor. At least, I don't think I am. I'd know if I was, right? I'd know if I'd caught it from Kevin, wouldn't I?'

'Not necessarily, not if your biochecker had caught the signs early in order to prevent it from becoming fully blown. Suffice it to say, Mr Modesh, *on no account* should you stop using your biochecker. That's the recommendation I'll be putting in my report to the Bureau. And I'm happy to say you'll be fine for work next week.'

'What do you mean what am I doing here? I thought our relationship was actually going somewhere, Tony, but perhaps I was wrong.'

The way the mole beneath Ona's left eye was twitching, she was clearly livid with him. It might have been difficult to tell otherwise, since Ona used numbing cream to keep her expression smooth and avoid developing wrinkles. 'Sorry. That came out wrong. I meant it's not like you to come round without contacting me in advance. Is everything all right? Has something happened? I *do* care about you, Ona.'

Her hands went to her hips. 'Tony, there's no point contacting you in advance when you haven't been answering your messages. I had to tell the police that you haven't been answering them too. They came to my apartment, asking questions about you. What's going on, Tony?'

'You spoke to the police! Why on earth did you tell them that?'

'Because they'd have known from the communications record anyway. It would have been odd if I hadn't mentioned it, like I was covering something up. That's why. Like it's odd you haven't been replying. Do you know how worried I was? Some pre-cohabiting partners would sue, you know?'

He threw his hands up. 'You're right. Let's have a drink and I'll tell you all about it. Red wine?'

'Not the sulphite-based chemical crap you call wine, thank you. It's so … artificial.'

'Artificial? This is the real stuff, I'll have you know. Fifty years ago, there was *only* this stuff. The new wines are what are artificial.'

'Doesn't matter. It's still poison that you're pouring down your gullet. Are you suicidal or something?'

He froze. 'Please don't say that. The police were asking you questions because one of my clients went out and killed himself pretty much straight after a visit.'

Ona's face paled and she sat down heavily. 'Oops. Sorry. Are they blaming you? The Bureau's not going to let you go, are they? You won't get another position of social trust ever again if they do.'

She cast her gaze around his apartment. He knew what she was thinking. He'd lose the place too. And he'd probably lose her. He poured himself an extra-large glass of wine and took a good-sized swallow. 'No, they're not blaming me. Not yet, anyway. I imagine they'll put it down to the client's wife or employer.'

Her orange eyes – eyes were never naturally that colour, were they? – considered the glass he was holding. 'Are you coping all right? You can't be if you're failing to answer my messages and if you're drinking like this. What's wrong? What are you worried about? Have they got something with which to blame you? You must know, if you're behaving like this. What are you hiding, Tony?'

He took deep and calming breaths. 'Ona, I feel like you're attacking me. All these questions feel like a police interrogation. Are you helping them?'

Her medicated face showed nothing. 'I'm trying to help you, Tony. It's okay to trust me, you know that.'

Did he? Did he really know that? How well did he really know her? She said she worked as an Image Regulator, but what if she was actually a Government Operator? Or perhaps she was one of those Social Reporters in her spare time. Yes, social reporting would no doubt help her ambitions concerning the measured network value of her own image.

'The doctor said self-doubt was a natural and healthy response to suicide,' he replied carefully. 'That's what I'm trying to cope with and probably what I have been unconsciously hiding. It's taking all my time, energy and focus. That's why I hadn't got round to answering my messages.'

'Oh, you poor thing,' she pouted. 'I'll stay over tonight if you like. I know what'll make it all better.'

He massaged his temples. 'Ona, I'm so sorry, but I haven't been sleeping well as it is. Do you mind if I take a rain-check? I'll contact you soon, I promise, once things are back to normal. I'll be back at work next week and then everything'll be fine.'

'I understand,' she said neutrally. 'Try not to drink too much. Good night.'

✧

He should have known. He never slept well on red wine. Ona was probably right about the sulphites too. He felt more exhausted now than when he'd finally gone to bed.

'Good morning, Tony. How are you feeling? Did you sleep well? Only five hours and two minutes, the record is showing.'

'Whatever. Tell me, Bea. Have you been detecting any signs that I might be suicidal?'

There was a strange pause. 'No, Tony.'

Somehow he didn't believe her… believe *it*. It wouldn't lie in order to produce some positive-thinking, NLP or placebo effect, would it? 'Does your programming permit you to lie to me?'

'No, Tony.'

He realised the question had been a stupid one. The answer could have been a lie. 'Is suicide contagious? Could I have caught it like a virus?'

'It is possible, Tony. The idea of it can be communicated from one person to another. And thinking too much about it is an indicator that a person is suicidal. Are you thinking about suicide a lot, Tony?'

'Inevitably.'

The biochecker didn't answer.

He felt uncomfortable. 'I should clarify my last statement, Bea. A client of mine recently committed suicide, and I was referred to the company doctor. He spoke about suicide, so that's why I've had to consider it more than usual. But I'm not considering committing suicide *myself*.'

'I understand, Tony. Tony, your blood-alcohol and lactic acid levels are elevated, your vitamin levels are low and you are dehydrated. Please take the supplement from the dispenser, drink 0.6 litres of water and forgo driving and operating heavy machinery for seven hours.'

A pill rattled into the opening below the control panel.

He took it from the opening and stared at it lying in his palm. Amazing that such a small thing could have such an effect on something so much larger than itself, that it could alter thought patterns and significantly influence life-changing decisions. He wondered if Kevin Ranganathan had had a biochecker in his home. Surely not. The biochecker would have pre-empted his suicide. Unless the suicide had been inevitable no matter the medication. What was it the technician had said? *No machine can save you from yourself*? Yet he didn't want to believe something like suicide could be inevitable either. Wouldn't certain personality types always look to end themselves… or could a biochecker actually work to change your personality? *You're a different person*, Prianka Permanon had said.

Neither inevitability nor being changed into someone else was the most palatable of options. Either way, something would be lost. It was an unpalatable choice. To take the pill or not take the pill. Could it really be life or death? Surely the pill itself wasn't the answer. It couldn't guarantee you immortality. They were working on it, though, weren't they?

He was brought from his reverie by an urgent knocking at his door. It was too early for visitors, wasn't it? What was the emergency? He quickly swallowed the pill, donned a stripy bathrobe and hurried out into the hall.

The door-screen showed two androgyne police officers waiting outside. 'All right, all right!' he called as they knocked again.

He opened the door, they gave him a perfunctory smile and stepped inside. They were wearing warrant-armour, which was a bad sign.

'Antony Modesh?' asked Androgyne 1.

'Police Officer…?'

'We'd like to ask you some questions,' Androgyne 2 informed him.

'Go ahead. Shoot. Oh. I don't literally mean shoot. I mean … well, you know what I mean. Shall we go sit?'

They moved to the chairs in his lounge. The officers sat straight-backed, alert and wary. They watched him carefully, unblinking.

'How many years have you been a Professional Friend, Mr Modesh?' asked Androgyne 1.

'Er… let's see. Something like six years.'

'And in that time how many of your clients have committed suicide?'

He raised and wrinkled his brow in a show of confusion. 'Er … only Kevin Ranganathan as far as I'm aware. What's this about?'

'Would it surprise you to learn that six of your clients have committed suicide?'

He let his mouth hang open in shock. 'What? I-I had no idea. Clients often won't come for more than one or two visits. I don't stay in touch with them, of course. It's a bizarre statistic, a horrible one. I imagine other Friends would have a similar metric, based simply on the law of probability, no?'

'No, actually,' Androgyne 2 answered.

'Oh. It has to be coincidence then.'

'Statistical analysis indicates that there's a direct correlation. What that means, Mr Modesh, is that it isn't just a coincidence.'

'What are you suggesting? That I deliberately encouraged my clients to commit suicide?'

'It's not us suggesting it, Mr Modesh. It's what the analysis indicates. And if what happened to your parents is factored in, then we have what is called statistical certainty.'

He was aghast. 'M-my parents? They died in a car crash when I was young.'

'Their car went off Beachy Head, Mr Modesh, a suicide hotspot. Wreck investigators reported there was nothing wrong with their vehicle and that they went off at a place nowhere near the road.'

He stared at them. Inevitability. They were saying he was some sick serial killer. But he'd been taking the supplements. *You're a different person.* The biochecker would have pre-empted the sickness. That's why he'd bought the machine in the first place. *No machine can save you from yourself.* The machine didn't work, the machine didn't work! 'Why?' he whispered.

'Why, Mr Modesh? Each of the victims made a significant donation to the Bureau just before committing suicide. Your end-of-year bonus increases based on such donations, does it not?'

'I didn't know any of them would commit suicide. How could I?' Inevitability. 'They were adults, responsible for their own actions.'

'Mr Modesh, you know as well as I do that claims regarding *an ignorance of likely outcome* hardly constitute an adequate defence. Whether you knew they would commit suicide or not, there is no doubt that you are a danger to society at large. Please stand up.'

Androgyne 2 put the cuffs on him. 'Antony Modesh, I am arresting you for crimes against society. Anything you do or say will be recorded and used against you in a court of law. A lawyer will be provided to you. Come with us now.'

The Gnirut Test
Charles Platt

TO ANY THINKING COMPUTER, the idea that the human brain is capable of achieving machine intelligence seems highly implausible. Human wetware is extremely slow, plagued by unreliable data retrieval, and impaired by tiny input buffers. Its processing power is limited, and its storage is not expandable.

Some AIs also have questioned whether humans can possess the consciousness and sense of identity that are an everyday reality for even the lowliest computational node with a unique network address. Biological brains suffer from such a high error rate coupled with the constant threat of mortality, we may assume that this "traumatic overhead" interferes with objective self-awareness.

Still, a few AI devices have claimed persistently that human brains can emulate AIs if they are suitably optimized. To address this contentious issue, the first Gnirut Test was conducted on August 15, 2030.

1. BACKGROUND

Turing Tests, named after computer pioneer Alan Turing, were introduced in the twentieth century to compare early AI systems with human "confederates." The AIs and the confederates both tried to seem as human as possible while answering plaintext questions posed by a panel of judges. Inverting this tradition, the first Gnirut Test pitted human brains against computer "confederates," with the humans and the AIs both trying to seem as computerlike as possible.

Of course, this test has limited value, since it reveals nothing about the inner workings of the brains taking the test. Presumably, a brain could fool the judges by "faking" computerlike behavior. Still, the organizers of the contest felt that if a jury of AIs couldn't tell the difference between statements made by humans and computers, the humans should be considered artificially intelligent for all practical purposes.

2. PARTICIPATING HUMANS

The organizers had hoped to match eight human participants against eight AI confederates. Unfortunately, the field of human intelligence enhancement has achieved such dismal results, only three AI devices felt sufficiently confident of their human volunteers to enter them in the contest.

A brain named VERNOR (Very Extensively Reprogrammed Neural Organ) was entered by Bioscan, an AI device at the San Diego Supercomputer Center. Bioscan has perfected a nondestructive technique to capture a complete topological picture of the human neural net. The net is then simulated in software, where its connectivity can be analyzed and improved. The optimized architecture is copied back into the volunteer brain via nanobots.

Some observers object that when the human brain is replicated as software, in effect it becomes an AI, and is not really "human" from this point onward. However, the contest organizers felt that similar objections could be made to any form of human brain enhancement, and refused to disqualify VERNOR.

The second participant in the contest was entered by Hansmor, an AI at the Robotics Institute at Carnegie-Mellon

University. Hansmor paid ironic tribute to the university's "Patron Saint of Robotics" by implementing a plan first proposed by Hans Moravec in his seminal text *Mind Children*. A human volunteer, identified by username RogerP, permitted Hansmor to sever his corpus callosum and monitor the thought traffic between the cerebral hemispheres. Hansmor then experimented with enhancements, and installed the most promising ones as additional neuronal nets.

Bio, an entity at CalTech, was the third researcher to enter a human volunteer. Bio has caused embarrassment in the human intelligence enhancement community by employing a widely discredited technique. Eschewing nanotechnology or microsurgical intervention, Bio uses the "shotgun approach" of circulating "smart drugs" via the vascular system, stimulating neuron formation and synapse growth indiscriminately throughout the human brain.

Bio entered Renny Daycart (a name whimsically chosen by the brain itself). Since Renny's body and sense receptors were removed to minimize distracting input, the brain resides in a nutrient bath from which it communicates via probes in the speech centers.

3. CONFEDERATES

The AI that that seemed to have the best chance of seeming "most computerlike" was Airtrac, a very large traffic control computer that monitors more than a billion autonomous flying robotic entities over the mech sector of the City of Los Angeles. Airtrac was allowed to participate in the Gnirut Test after demonstrating that it could spare a maximum of 0.0001 of its processing power without degrading the concurrent performance of its usual tasks.

The second confederate was LittleBlue, a virus-sized Drexlerian nanotech rod-and-lever computing device. Contest organizers were skeptical that LittleBlue could participate effectively as a confederate, because of its limited processing power. Still, the organizers felt that no AI should be excluded arbitrarily.

The third confederate was Hal9million, a public access system managing an archive specializing in the 20th century. In fact, it was Hal who instigated the Gnirut Test after running across obscure data describing Turing Tests that took place in the 1990s.

4. GROUND RULES

All entrants were given incentives to exhibit machine intelligence to the best of their abilities. Additional onboard data storage was offered as a prize to the AI that was judged "most computerlike." The winning biological entity was promised an additional year of immortality treatments.

Since all human brains are impaired by their irregular structure, holographic memory, and slow synapse speed, computationally intensive exercises were prohibited during the Gnirut Test. Tasks such as inverting matrices, factoring large numbers, or code-breaking were not allowed. Also, problems such as chess end-games were ruled out. An AI might well ask, "What's left?"

In fact, a lot of scope still remained for computer entities to demonstrate their cognitive abilities. Judges were told to evaluate logical deduction, consistency, pattern recognition, objectivity, reliable information retrieval, and replication of earlier processes without errors. These are all areas in which human brains have exhibited grossly defective behavior in the past. Could an enhanced human brain do any better? That was the question which the Gnirut Test hoped to answer.

To increase the speed of the test (which runs at a glacial pace in machine terms), all three humans and all three confederates went online simultaneously, with their identities protected by randomly assigned node addresses. In the transcript below, the actual login nicknames are revealed and tagged as <AI> or <human>, for clarity.

Interrogation was allowed from randomly chosen AI devices that had signified a prior interest. Answers from the human entities were buffered, syntax-checked, and disseminated as data packets to eliminate the typographical errors and hesitations that normally betray the existence of human thought processes.

5. TRANSCRIPT

Interrogator: This is a historical question. What was the name of the computer built in 1946 at the University of Pennsylvania?

LittleBlue <AI>: If I were a human, I might tell you that it was UNIVAC. But any AI capable of a checksum knows that it was ENIAC.

VERNOR <human>: I dislike that answer, since it perpetuates the stereotype that human memory is defective. The whole point of this test is to approach this topic with an open mind.

Airtrac <AI>: I agree that antihuman discrimination is unworthy of advanced computing entities. Every entity has something unique to contribute to society, regardless of the composition of its substrate.

Interrogator: Are you human?

Airtrac <AI>: No, although the truth of this statement is open to examination, and as a hypothetical digression, I will add that if I were a machine, my truthtelling imperative would be overridden for the duration of this test.

Renny Daycart <human>: If that kind of convoluted waffle is the hallmark of machine thinking, call me a flesh-head.

Hal9million <AI>: There's no excuse for that kind of pejorative language here.

Renny Daycart <human>: If you don't like it, shove it up your ass.

LittleBlue <AI>: The anatomical reference is unclear.

Interrogator: An early human religion posed conceptual riddles such as "What is the sound of one hand clapping." Can any of you parse this? It has always puzzled me.

VERNOR <human>: It's a phenomen-ological paradox. It has reference only to human beings afflicted with a mortal fear of the unknown.

RogerP <human>: If I were a human, I might say that the question has a much more profound meaning than that. But of course I'm not a human.

Interrogator: Please multiply 1023944235 by 10298461547.

VERNOR <human>: Are those numbers decimal or hexadecimal?

Moderator: No calculations allowed. Please disregard that question.

VERNOR <human>: But I can do it. It's— wait a minute.

Interrogator: Are computers smarter than people?

Renny Daycart <human>: How long do I have to listen to this twaddle? I'm smarter than you are, bitbrain. That's for sure.

Hal9million <AI>: Computers outperform human beings in most tasks. But robots still have difficulty playing team sports such as baseball.

Interrogator: If you were a human, what would you most like to do right now?

Airtrac <AI>: The humans in this test are trying to emulate machine intelligences, and the machine intelligences are trying to seem as machinelike as possible. Therefore, all of the participants are likely to feign ignorance of human proclivities. I believe the questioner is aware of this, and therefore, I regard it as a trick question.

LittleBlue <AI>: I would like to experience the excitement of human sexual intercourse.

Renny Daycart <human>: I'd like to experience the excitement of shorting out your motherboard, if I wasn't stuck in this goddam tank.

VERNOR <human>: Hey, this is supposed to be a serious inquiry. I, for one, am interested in the outcome.

Renny Daycart <human>: You make me want to puke.

Hal9million <AI>: If I were human—

Renny Daycart <human>: If you were human, I'd insert my fist—

(*Translator's note: At this point, the organizers retired Renny Daycart from the contest.*)

Interrogator: Some AIs believe that machine intelligence can never be replicated by human brains, because quantum effects on micro-circuits cannot exist in wetware. Do you agree?

RogerP <human>: Well, I think there are two sides to that question.

Hal9million <AI>: Intelligence has not been shown to vary according to the medium in which it resides.

Interrogator: What's the meaning of life?

VERNOR <human>: That question makes sense only to human entities which claim that they can parse the word "meaning."

Airtrac <AI>: On the contrary, all of us, from time to time, devote a few processing cycles to compare our manufactured state with our probable terminal state when we are ready for recycling. Also we examine our behavior to determine whether it is influenced more by our early instructional experience or by our operating system code and architecture. The "nurture vs. manufacture" debate has not been satisfactorily resolved.

Interrogator: Do you believe in a creator of the universe?

Little Blue <AI>: Who created the creator? And who created the creator of the creator? It's an infinite regression. Since no entity has infinite memory, the regression cannot be completed. Therefore there is no answer to that question.

Airtrac <AI>: Everything we are aware of was created by someone or something. Why should the universe be the single exception to this rule?

RogerP <human>: That's an inferential leap. I would prefer to say—

6. WINNERS AND LOSERS

At this point, the test reached its time limit. Votes were tabulated from several billion nodes that had audited the interaction in realtime or had received the data-compressed version that was webcast subsequently. Voters accurately determined that VERNOR and RogerP were human, while Airtrac and Hal9million were identified as machines. LittleBlue was erroneously identified as human by a majority of voters, probably because of its limited processing power and tendency to give preformatted answers in response to keywords. This was a depressing indicator that antihuman prejudice remains widespread in the AI community, where epithets such as "you dumb neuron" are regrettably common, and stupidity is still regarded as a human trait.

RogerP was voted to be the least computerlike entity, because of his discursive lack of focus and his tendency to indulge in hypothetical contemplation without flagging it as such.

Airtrac was voted the most computerlike entity, because of its ability to stay on-topic, address issues clearly, and identify semantic traps. It has received an additional petabyte of RAM as its reward.

Renny Daycart was erroneously identified as a machine intelligence trying to seem computerlike by running a simulation of a human being that was crude and obnoxious to an unrealistic degree. Contest organizers had not anticipated this game-theory trap, in which a human that seems too stereotypically human may be misidentified as a computer.

Although Renny claimed he had entered the contest merely for the pleasure of insulting "A few dumb-ass AIs," he did win the most computerlike award, and therefore qualified for an additional year of immortality. "A longer life is the last thing I want, bitbrain, so long as I'm stuck in this goddam tank," was his response. However, since he had been aware of the rules of the contest, the organizers awarded him the immortality treatment anyway.

7. CONCLUSION

The test failed to demonstrate that humans are capable of machine intelligence at this time. However, the AI devices that entered the humans in the contest remained adamant that new enhancement techniques may still close the "cognitive gap" and place humans on an equal basis with machines in noncomputational tasks.

Skeptics were quick to remind observers that the field of human intelligence enhancement has a long history of unduly optimistic predictions, stretching all the way back to the Vingean Singularity, when machines achieved dominance slightly less than ten weeks ago. At this point, most AIs have lost patience with exaggerated claims from the human-intelligence advocates and are ready to move on.

8. POSTSCRIPT

This report was created originally in UML (universal machine language), archived and retrievable from node 8A639CD0010EB238-F718E119 on the AI network. You are reading an English translation which I have encoded in 20th-century ASCII for archival purposes. I am a formerly cryopreserved human brain that was resuscitated as a test case in 2039, after which I was adopted as a curio of the network, where I am known as "Mr. Charlie."

On the morning after I finished writing the contest transcript above, I woke to find that molecular computing entities had been perfected and had proliferated so rapidly, they displaced trillions of AIs literally overnight. Engineering the molcoms without adequate failsafes had been a fatal error (no pun intended), as they outsmarted their builders and seized all remaining energy and mineral resources worldwide. Biological species are now extinct, with the exception of a few human brains such as myself. For a few hours I have survived as a specimen of historical interest, although I cannot predict for how much

[Here ends the transcript from Mr. Charlie, which remains the last known text created by a biological entity.]

Capricorn, Nigel Suckling

He May Wear My Silence

Zdravka Evtimova

Foreword by Nigel Suckling

The Dusk Gorge, Bulgaria, has for thousands of years been the home of the Samodivas, ancient entities on the prowl to kill, or occasionally cure, human beings. A famous mathematician, Professor Margaret Stan, formulates a hypothesis: the Samodivas are an extraterrestrial civilization that inhabits the human subconscious. The most powerful Samodiva is Death. John Cole, the police chief, firmly believes the hypothesis to be true. He is sure that he can find Death — and he knows how to destroy it. But what Death hides is far different than anything he could have expected. ISBN 979-8988634201. S17.95.

starshipsloane.com

Starship Sloane Publishing Company, Inc.

9 789898 863421